A Warrior's Touch
A Novella of the Pruxnæ

Lucy Varna

Bone Diggers Press
www.bonediggerspress.com

For Caleb

Cover design © S. Frost Designs.

Published by Bone Diggers Press, Clayton, Georgia.

ISBN 978-1-943465-16-3

PRAISE FOR THE NOVELS
OF LUCY VARNA

The Prophecy
"Varna cleverly layers romance and mystery on top of adventure without detriment to any of the genres."
—*Reading to Distraction*

Light's Bane
"A fast paced and exciting read."
--*Paranormal, Magic and Mischief*

The Enemy Within
"The writing is solid and engaging, and the plot moved fast from start to end."
--*Forever Book Lover*

"The setting and world-building is brilliant. It's a magnificent world, with its own customs and rules, and it all makes sense somehow."
--*I Heart Reading*

Tempered
"If you love tough heroines you are going to adore Hawthorne."
--*Cryptic Reads*

"*Tempered* is the kind of book that makes you want to read the rest in the series. What's better than that?"
--*Dark Writer*

TITLES BY LUCY VARNA

THE DAUGHTERS OF THE PEOPLE SERIES
The Prophecy
Light's Bane
The Enemy Within
Tempered
In All Things, Balance
Sanctuary

THE SONS OF THE PEOPLE SERIES
Say Yes

THE PRUXNÆ SERIES
Thief of Hearts
The Choosing
Alien Mine

THE CULLOWHEE HERITAGE SERIES
A Higher Purpose
A Wicked Love

COMING SOON

Sweet Surrender
(A Novel of the Pruxnæ)

The Gathering Storm
(Daughters of the People, Book 6)

Visit www.lucyvarna.com for more information.

CHAPTER ONE

YASMIN OLVERA curled up on her sofa with a fresh cup of hot cocoa cupped between her hands. A fire burned brightly in the insert installed in the creek rock fireplace. It was snowing outside, a rare treat as the seasons neared the change from fall into winter. She loved the snow, loved watching it fall, loved being outside in the crisp air and catching snowflakes on her tongue as they drifted to the earth. Just the thought of it should make her happy.

Somehow, though, it was simply one more misery among a year of unhappiness.

Yasmin blew gently across the top of her cocoa. There'd been too many changes over the past few months. Most of them had come about after Marty Benfield had broken off their engagement. Him, she didn't miss at all. He could keep his archaic notions about immigration to himself, thank you very much, and she'd be just fine not having to explain repeatedly something he already knew, that she was the second generation of her family to be born in the States and a successful businesswoman in her own right.

It should've been enough. If he'd loved her, maybe it would've been, but he hadn't. Otherwise, he wouldn't have shed her faster than a NASCAR driver at Talladega when her brother's old gang started making trouble.

That trouble had chased Yasmin's best friend, Rachel Hunter, right off Earth and halfway around the galaxy, along with her daughters and Rachel's handsome fiancé, Dyuvad ab Mhij, a man who'd been born on another planet. Talk about a whopper of a surprise. To think, there really was intelligent life living among the stars, and some of it was human.

The fire hissed and popped. Yasmin sipped her cocoa, savoring the rich chocolate creaminess, and sighed. Mmm, perfect. Maybe everything in her life wasn't great, but she had a solid business, built by her own hands into the best florist in the county, and she had her health. A lot of people couldn't say the same.

Then again, a lot of people weren't greeted first thing in the morning by mauled animals left on their front porches.

A shiver snaked down Yasmin's spine. She really had to figure out what to do about that, and soon.

At least she couldn't blame Marty for that little mess.

The porch creaked outside her front door, and Yasmin's heart leapt into her throat. She glanced at the clock on the mantel. Ten eighteen, far too late for visitors. Surely it was too early for *them* to leave their little surprises, though.

She set her cocoa on the coffee table and grabbed the aluminum baseball bat Rachel's brother, Fate, had insisted she keep, in lieu of the gun he'd given her that she hadn't a clue how to use. It didn't have to be trouble outside. An animal could've wandered onto the porch. A bear, maybe. Fate had spotted one a couple of weeks back and warned her to keep a wary eye out for it.

The porch's aging floorboards creaked again.

Yasmin's hands tightened on the grip of the bat. Sure, that's what it was. A bear, searching for its last meal before it crawled into a cave and slept 'til spring.

Something heavy hit the front door, and Yasmin shrieked. She clapped a hand over her mouth and backed slowly away. Whatever was out there, it wasn't a bear, unless bears had started standing upright and knocking on the door.

She inhaled slowly, then dropped her hand. "Who's there?"

"Benar Q'Mhel," a gruff voice said.

Yasmin sagged against the sofa's cushioned arm. Dyuvad had promised he'd send his brother to check on her, but that had been weeks ago. She'd forgotten all about the famed mercenary-soldier in the meantime. Who wouldn't, with the holidays and everything else going on?

She kept a firm grip around the bat, just in case, scurried to the door, and swung it open on a man dressed in a black, chest-hugging turtleneck tucked into sturdy, black cargo pants under a knee-length leather coat. Hard, midnight blue eyes, completely devoid of expression above high cheekbones, stared down at her from inches above her own head. His nose was sharper than Dyuvad's and not quite as wide, but his cheeks had the same hollow look of a sculpture and a little dimple softened his chin, exactly like his younger brother's.

Their hair was different, though. Dyuvad kept his short. This man had twisted his black locks into a stubby ponytail at the nape of his neck. Two thin braids hung from his left temple, adding a rakish hint to his dangerous aura.

He shifted his hold on the strap of the black duffel slung across his shoulder. "Lady Yasmin?"

The last of Yasmin's nerves faded. She loosened her grip on the bat and leaned it against the wall beside the front door. This man had to be Dyuvad's brother or somebody from the same planet. No man on Earth was polite enough to call a woman *lady* unless she'd earned the title, and sometimes not even then.

She stepped aside and motioned Benar in, then closed the door behind him, shutting out the cold. "I hope those clothes are warmer than they look."

"They are."

The words were as flat as his eyes. They dropped into the space between them, so heavy, Yasmin could just about hear each syllable hitting the hardwood floor.

She cleared her throat and tried again. "Would you like something to eat or drink? Some cocoa, maybe. I just made some and—"

"Stop."

She closed her mouth around her offer of hospitality.

"Show me your abode."

"Sure," she said slowly. "Why am I showing you my house?"

His impassive gaze swept once around the great room, then

landed on her. "How many other rooms are there?"

"Two bedrooms, two bathrooms, a pantry, and a laundry room." She pointed at the ceiling. "A half attic upstairs. Look, Dyuvad said—"

Benar's hand shot out and gripped her upper arm. "Where are the exits?"

His gloved fingers were gentle, holding her firmly. Yasmin tugged at her arm and got exactly nowhere. "This and the door leading out of my bedroom onto the back porch are it. Can I have my arm back now?"

"Show me the back exit."

"Kinda need my arm for that," she muttered.

He arched an imperious, black eyebrow. "Show me the exit now, woman."

Well, that sealed it. This man was definitely related to Rachel's fiancé. Domineering Dyuvad had stepped in and saved Rachel's bacon, but he'd done it exactly the way he'd wanted to, without thought or consideration for the fact that it was Rachel's bacon to save, not his.

Yasmin jerked her arm out of Benar's grip and stuck her chin out. So what if it was her bacon in the fire now? This mess was hers and hers alone, and she could handle it without a high and mighty alien warrior getting in her way.

Couldn't she?

BENAR Q'MHEL stared down at the Earth woman, mildly amused by the determined set of her square chin. She was thin and willowy, her delicate features creamy and exotic, even by his standards, and was obviously incompetent to handle herself. Otherwise, Dyuvad would not have pressed Benar to visit this backwater planet and protect the woman.

A shame. If she had more backbone, he'd consider taking her as his lover. She was attractive enough, for a Terran, but no son of the strong-willed Mhij Ak would ever be happy with a weak woman. Still, she was there and ripe for the taking, and he'd been a long time without.

4

Yasmin jerked her arm out of his grip. "Dyuvad tried that *I'm the boss* crap on Rachel. It didn't get him any farther with her than you'll get using it on me."

His lips twitched. By Wode, at least she had some gumption. He snagged her elbow, ignoring her sharp slaps and futile attempts to dislodge his hold, and spun her toward the back of her home. "The exit. The next time I have to ask, it'll be with my hand spanking your ass."

Her eyes narrowed into sharp, dark slits. "Try it and you'll draw back a nub."

He bit back a bark of laughter. As if a woman half his weight could hurt him, especially one without the skills to defend herself.

"Maybe two," she added, and tossed her head, bouncing the nearly black curls pinned into a messy bun on her crown. "Insufferable lout. The exit's this way."

She led him through the room between a sitting area surrounding a decorated evergreen and fireplace on the left and a kitchen on the right, into a short hallway. He pulled her to a stop between two doors, one leading into an immaculately kept bedroom, the other into a small room with lavender walls.

"Guest bedroom and bath," she said. "No outside exits unless you count the bedroom's windows."

He grunted and urged her toward the last remaining door, into a large bedroom occupying the width of the cabin. A fireplace and a good-sized bed covered in a muted floral print were on the left. Two doors were on the right. He peeked into each, dragging a protesting Yasmin with him. The first held another bathing chamber, this one with pale yellow walls and a large, claw-footed tub. The other room held rows of clothing organized by type and color.

Yasmin pointed with her free hand to a door on the opposite side of the room from the hallway. "There's the back exit. Now let me go."

He maneuvered her toward the bed and pushed her onto its end, then dropped his carryall onto the floor at her feet. "Stay here, woman."

Her brown eyes flashed fire. "Stay here, show me the exit," she

5

muttered. "If Dyuvad had acted like this, Rachel would've given him the boot first thing."

"I'm not my brother." And he was happy the way he was, as his youngest brother was happy being himself.

Benar turned his back on the woman's pouting, ignoring it for what it was, a weak attempt to control him, and examined the door. Like the front entrance, it was solid wood and had a locking handle and a sturdy deadbolt. He turned the metal knob and yanked, and grunted when the frame creaked. A good-sized man could break it down with some effort and enough determination.

"Who wishes to harm you?" he asked.

Yasmin sniffed her slender nose. "I don't see how that's any of your concern, Mr. Q'Mhel."

"Q'Mhel," he corrected. "No mister. Answer the question."

"Didn't Dyuvad tell you?"

"Only that someone was harassing you and you're unable to protect yourself."

Her eyes dropped to the black slacks she wore. She cupped her knees and squeezed until the skin covering her knuckles whitened. "I can protect myself."

He grunted. Obviously not. "We're sleeping on my ship tonight."

Her eyes flew up and grew round. "I'm not letting a bunch of hooligans run me out of my own home."

"Answer my question and maybe I will allow you to stay."

"Allow me..." Her mouth snapped shut and she shoved herself off the bed. "Now, you listen here, Benar Q'Mhel. Nobody lets me do anything. I have a business to run and a life to live, and I'm not letting a domineering Neanderthal from outer space tell me how to do either."

He crossed the distance between them in two long strides and yanked her against his chest. "You will do as I say, woman. If I say we leave, you'll go and be happy about it. Is that clear?"

She smacked a balled up fist against his stomach. "Bully."

"Protector."

Her scent washed over him, something light and spicy and

intoxicating. He hitched her another inch higher and lowered his head, breathing her in. She was light against him, delicate, and tempting. Against his better judgment, his body stirred to life and the first thrum of desire throbbed through his blood. It had been a long time since he'd been with a woman, months of duty and work relieved by precious few moments of recreation. He was protecting the woman anyway. Why not take her as his lover?

Her eyes dropped to his mouth and her breath hitched in, and when she spoke, her voice was wispy thin. "What are you doing?"

"Measuring your worth." An honest enough statement, though it wasn't the complete truth. He eased her away from him and stepped back, letting temptation go. "Lock the door behind me."

"You're leaving?"

"Perimeter sweep. Stay inside."

He unlocked the pitifully insecure back door and stepped through its narrow frame onto a screened-in porch half the length of the cabin, braced against an addition to the right. He opened the unlocked door into the extra room and discovered two white, metal machines, closed it with a grim shake of his head. The woman was going to be more trouble than she was worth. The knowledge was an uneasy ache in his gut, extending deep into his bones. Nothing good would come of protecting her. Still, he'd promised Dyuvad he'd watch over her until her troubles passed, and a Q'Mhel never backed down on his word.

Benar retrieved the gun holstered against his lower back and stepped into the night, shedding his unease as quickly as it had come.

CHAPTER TWO

YASMIN READIED FOR BED with unsteady hands and a thready heartbeat. Benar had been gone for half an hour at least, long enough for her to set out fresh towels for him and plump the pillows on the spare bed. A guest was a guest, regardless of his attitude, and he would be treated hospitably during his stay.

Arrogant, know it all jerk.

She slammed a pillow onto the bed and glared at it. What was it about testosterone that made a man think he could throw his weight around? Honestly, it was as if having hair on his chest gave Benar the right to treat every woman like she was his personal slave.

She lowered her voice to a soft, guttural imitation of Benar's and muttered, "Show me the exit, woman. Stay and be a good girl, woman."

"I never told you to be a good girl."

Yasmin gasped and whirled around, one hand on her heart. Benar stood in the doorway, snowflakes melting on his leather jacket, expression as impassive as stone. His dark eyes slid down her pajama clad body and landed on her garnet colored toenails.

She tucked one bare foot behind her leg, hiding five toes in worn, snowman patterned flannel. What had ever possessed her to buy a nail polish called Limited Addiction? And why hadn't she remembered the alluring color when she'd changed into her pajamas?

Benar's eyes flicked up to hers and one corner of his mouth twitched. "Be naughty if you want, but do it when I don't need you to obey me."

"Obey..." She huffed out an infuriated breath. "What gives you the right to tell me what to do?"

"I do."

He stripped his gloves off and tossed them onto the bed as he strolled toward her, all lean grace and deadly intent, and his expression wasn't impassive anymore. It was taut, needy. His gaze raked over her again, hot and knowing, and his lips, so cruel and hard before, softened into a small smile.

Yasmin held out a hand in a futile attempt to stave him off. She didn't want him there in her home, consuming space she'd rather save for someone she liked. And she sure didn't like that smile, the way it brightened him from the inside out, the way it sparked through her, leaving a trail of heat in its wake.

He walked right into her hand and kept going, stopping when they were so close she could feel his body heat, and captured her hand between one calloused palm and his firm chest. "Are you ready for bed?"

"Almost."

"Help me undress."

She shook her head. Southern hospitality did not extend to undressing sexy strangers. "Forget it. You're a grown man. Do it yourself."

He grinned, quick and sure. "Scared?"

"Hardly," she scoffed. "I have to finish getting ready for bed. You can sleep here, by the way. The sheets are clean and—"

His hand shot out, quick as a snake striking, and curled around her upper arm, holding her in place. "Undress me."

She choked on an inhaled breath. "I already said no, and when a woman says no—"

He yanked her against him, holding her there with one hand and a determined curl of his lips. "I've warned you once, woman. The next time I tell you to do something and you refuse, I'll spank your ass."

"Oh, you...*brute*!" she sputtered. "This isn't the Middle Ages and I am not your lapdog. Take off your own clothes."

His eyes narrowed into thin, hot slits. "You're disobeying me."

"Darn tootin'."

"Then you leave me no choice."

He bent and, before she could utter another protest, slung her over his left shoulder, knocking the air out of her lungs. She wheezed in a labored breath as he strode out of the room, his left arm curved firmly around the back of her thighs, her upper body bouncing against his back.

Madre de Dios, the man was insane.

She braced a palm against his waist and whacked him with a balled up fist. "Put me down, you cretin."

He smacked her bottom hard, stinging her skin through her thin pajama bottoms and panties. "Struggling will only make it worse."

Worse? How could it possibly be worse? She was dangling upside down across an alien's shoulder, with her bottom up in the air and his hand caressing the spot he'd smacked. It was downright undignified.

"Is this what you tell the people you go after?" she asked. "Don't struggle. I'll only kill you faster?"

"I usually kill them outright. Then I don't have to say anything."

He dropped her unceremoniously onto her bed, then followed her down. She kicked and bucked and resisted every effort he made to turn her over, but in the end, she lay flat on her stomach crosswise over her duvet, breathless, with him straddling her thighs, pinning her to the bed.

She buried her face in the duvet. "Don't you dare spank me."

"Concede and I will stay my hand."

"I told you. I'm not your lapdog."

"No. You're a beautiful woman, desirable." His hand came down on her bottom, not quite as hard as before, and lingered there, caressing her. "Don't move."

Heat spiraled through her, radiating away from his touch. She groaned into the duvet. Great. She'd just kicked one jerk out of her life, and here was another one. Only, this one was tall and handsome and hotter than sin, and he was sitting in her bedroom fondling her like she was already his.

She fumbled through her dwindling reason for a rational response. "I can't move with you on top of me. Why don't you get off so I can turn over and punch you for groping me?"

He laughed, low and soft and husky. "I like your spirit, woman."

"That's not all you're gonna like in a minute," she muttered. "I need to bank the fire."

"Later."

His weight eased off her and was gone in the soft swish of his legs sliding across her duvet and the mattress shifting as he stood. She promptly rolled over, just in time to watch Benar shrug out of his jacket. She scooted to the edge of the bed and held out a hand. "I'll hang that up for you."

"Now you choose to obey, after your punishment is already nigh?" He clucked his tongue once and draped his jacket over the hope chest positioned at the end of her bed. "Too late, beauty."

She bit her tongue on a rude retort. Hospitality. She really had to remember that he was her guest and a stranger to Earth. And that he was her best friend's future brother-in-law. Rachel would kill her if anything happened to Benar.

Like, for example, him having an aluminum baseball bat applied forcefully to the side of his hard head.

"You're my guest," she said evenly. "You don't know where anything is in my house."

"Show me tomorrow."

He yanked his turtleneck out of the waistband of his jeans and pulled it over his head, and Yasmin's mouth went dry. His chest was leanly muscled and covered with a fine mat of black hair, tapering into a line leading straight down his torso past his belly button, where it disappeared into his jeans. He wore a thin choker filled with tiny, multi-colored beads encircling his strong neck, but what drew her attention were the fine, almost invisible scars bisecting his smooth, sun burnished skin.

She sucked in a ragged breath, her impossible attraction to him forgotten. So many scars, a lifetime worth, but he couldn't be old enough to have earned so many, could he? His face was barely wrinkled, still full of the vibrancy of youth, even if his eyes were as cold as the night sky.

"How old are you?" she blurted out, and nearly winced. His rudeness didn't justify her own. She opened her mouth to apologize for the question, and was surprised when he spoke.

"In Earth years? About twenty-seven. Why?"

"No reason." She jerked her eyes away from that fabulous chest and focused on the bedroom doorway. "You should really undress in the guest room."

"We're sleeping in here."

Her eyes flew to his. "You are not sleeping in my bed."

"I am."

"Fine. *I'll* sleep in the guest room."

He leaned down until their faces were inches apart and snagged her chin, tilting it toward his. "Let us be clear, Yasmin. As long as I am here acting as your protector, you will do what I tell you and you will do it quickly. Your security is dependent upon me being close by, ready to act against any aggression. Do you truly wish to face your tormenter alone? If so, I will leave now and forsake my promise to Dyuvad."

A thin tendril of fear snaked down her spine. Well, if he put it like that, how could she object to him sleeping beside her? It wasn't for long, right? And there was plenty of room in the Queen-sized sleigh bed for both of them, as long as they each kept to their own side.

True, it was her bacon to save, but why do it alone when she had a perfectly good warrior at her beck and call?

"All right," she conceded. "You can stay, but don't get any ideas."

He brushed his mouth across hers, a fleeting caress. "I already have ideas, beauty, and you will enjoy every one of them."

Heat flared in her blood and her pussy throbbed, and she inwardly cursed. After all the crap Marty had put her through, she should've learned her lesson. And yet here she was, allowing a sexy stranger to ensnare her with his dirty little plans.

He released her chin and sauntered toward the bathroom, giving her a fine view of his strong back and firmly muscled bottom. She flopped back on the bed and stared up at the ceiling, torn between the sensual promise in his husky voice and the urge to run screaming in the opposite direction. Eight days until Christmas. Surely Benar would figure out who was harassing her before then and be on his way, and she could enjoy the holidays surrounded by her family and friends, once again alone.

A VIBRATION in his left wrist woke Benar from a light sleep. He came alert instantly, senses tuned to the slightest sound. Yasmin was asleep beside him, curled into a ball with her head on his bicep and her knees tucked against his stomach.

She'd started out on the opposite side of the cushy bed, her stiff back turned toward him. As the room's air had chilled, she'd steadily crept across the bed under the layers of blankets, lured by his warmth and the security of his presence, and snuggled into him.

As a lover should.

Wood creaked from the direction of the front room. Benar turned toward it, careful not to rouse Yasmin. *Time*, he thought, and ignored a slight twinge as the information was fed into his brain by the neural net implanted in his left temple. Five eighteen local time, hours before sunrise. It could be the house settling. It could be wildlife helping themselves to the shelter offered by Yasmin's porches.

Or it could be those intent on harming her.

His gut tightened as years of training and instinct kicked in. *Sensor sweep, infrared*, he thought as he eased away from Yasmin and out of bed. He pulled the covers over her shoulders, retrieved his gun from the nightstand where he'd placed it earlier, and padded nude through her house, his bare feet silent against the wooden floors.

The creak sounded again, followed by a scuffle and a hissed curse. The sensor sweep flooded into Benar's mind, highlighting him, Yasmin, and a solitary, humanoid figure moving rapidly away from her home.

Benar broke into a run and twisted the door open. Frigid air hit his skin, chilling him to the core. A dissected animal lay on the stoop, steam wafting off its freshly exposed entrails. Benar stepped over it and shut the door behind himself, his eyes scanning the yard dimly illuminated by a street lamp some thirty ceg distant. A door slammed beyond the circle of light, breaking the night's stillness. An engine revved, and faded as it moved away from Yasmin's house on the paved street linking her driveway to the world beyond.

Benar stared at the space where the unknown vehicle had likely disappeared. Whoever had left an offering for Yasmin was familiar enough with her property to know how to get on and off of it with little trouble. They'd known where to place the mutilated animal, where to hide their getaway, and the quickest route in between. Anyone could've gathered that intel with enough time and patience. That the harasser held that information didn't prove anything. Yet.

He spun on the ball of his foot and reentered the house, snapping silent orders through his relay. He needed to see the sensor sweep again, preferably on his ship's bridge, and he needed more security around Yasmin's home. Daylight was soon enough for either.

In the meantime, there was no need for Yasmin to see the animal sacrificed to her tormenter's pleasure. Benar pulled on his clothes in her darkened bedroom and scrounged through his carryall for a folding shovel. It wouldn't take long to bury the creature. Hours remained yet for holding his new prize, and he intended to enjoy every moment of her sleep softened body.

Yasmin stretched, rustling the sheets, and pushed herself off her pillow. "Benar?"

He sat down on the edge of the bed and smoothed a stray curl away from her exquisite features. "Go back to sleep, beauty. I won't be long."

She flopped onto the pillow, eyes closed. "Ok."

He kissed her forehead softly and left, half of his mind turned toward his duty, the other half pondering his new conquest. A day or two for her to become accustomed to his presence, and then, he'd coax her into love play, and pleasure her far more surely than any man had before.

Chapter Three

YASMIN WOKE surrounded by the heat of an unfamiliar, male body. She stiffened reflexively, and then her brain kicked in and delivered memories of the night before. Benar, sexy mercenary-soldier and all around domineering Neanderthal, was in bed with her. He'd insisted, the lout, and maybe he'd been right to. It was the first night since the incidents had started that she'd slept well.

He stirred behind her and pressed his rock hard erection into her bottom. "Myengen dun arig, Yasmin."

She resisted conflicting urges to either rub her bottom against his arousal or ease away from him. Less than twenty-four hours into knowing him and he was already driving her crazy. And wasn't that just like a man?

"What does that mean?" she asked.

"Good morning. Say it."

"Good morning?"

His hand slid down her side and curved around her hip, and he pulled her bottom firmly into the crook of his body. "In Pruxnæ. Myengen dun arig. Say it."

"Ah, myengen dun arig."

He laughed into her hair, low and soft, stirring the fine strands. "You're learning."

The hot burn of her Latina temper flashed through her. Smug, infuriating male. Why had she given in to him?

"Don't get any ideas," he said. "I'm not finished with you yet."

"*You* don't get any ideas," she hissed. "Just because you're here helping me, that doesn't mean I'm having sex with you."

"Yes, it does. Turn over onto your back."

"I'm not—"

In no time flat, he maneuvered her onto her back and covered her body with his, buried his face in her hair and cradled his sex against hers. For one brief, insane moment, she allowed herself to enjoy his weight and the slow rub of his erection across her core through her panties, the gentle puff of his breath into her ear, the kiss he pressed to her temple. She'd never woken up with a man before, never lain with one in her bed, and it was delicious, tempting. Heat curled through her, steady and insistent, and her pussy throbbed in time to his hips rocking into hers. This was what tempted women into sin, this pleasure threading into her blood, the promise of more in the sensual flex of his body.

So much temptation.

She stiffened and shoved at his shoulders. No, she wouldn't give in, not with a near stranger. She'd resisted Marty's best efforts to bed her for years, and he'd been her fiancé. Why should she allow Benar to take what was hers and hers alone to share?

"Get off me, you heathen," she said, and was appalled at the weak huff of words she'd meant to be defiant, tough.

He laughed again, a husky whisper of sound. "When I'm finished."

"I'm not having sex with you."

"You're the only one talking about sex." He slid down her body half a foot and nuzzled the pulse throbbing in her throat. "Mmm. If we were lovers, I'd mark you here so everyone would know who you belong to."

She smacked his bare shoulder, and was somewhat mollified by the satisfying slap echoing in the room. "I belong to myself, thank you. Now get off. I have to go to work."

"In a tick."

His mouth covered her pulse again and sucked lightly, and the desire lingering within her flared to life with the roar and fury of a hurricane. She bit her lower lip in a futile attempt to stifle it.

Too late.

16

Her hips shot up of their own accord, seeking the relief of his touch, and she cursed their betrayal. Stupid, sex-starved body. If she'd known this was the way she'd react to the first handsome alien to show up on her doorstep, she would've given in to Marty. Or not. He'd never made her feel like this, electric and alive, every nerve burning under the sensate skill of his lips on her skin. Twenty-eight years was a long time to live without experiencing passion so wondrous. Too bad it had taken a gang-lead threat and an alien army of one for her to know it.

Benar shifted over her and kissed the other side of her neck, exactly opposite his first one, then resumed his original position on top of her. "Myengen dun arig, yarl Yasmin."

"Good morning, Benar."

He clucked his tongue as he rolled off her and out of bed, and padded across the room, naked as the day he'd been born. She pointedly fixed her eyes on the ceiling, ignoring the glacially slow seep of desire inside her and the beautifully formed length of his body. Just seven days until Christmas, six more nights of him beside her in bed. Surely she could hold out that long without giving in to temptation. Surely, she could.

THE SHOP was unusually busy that day. Yasmin centered herself in the midst of the bustle of customers and staff, and managed the flow of both with a velvet-gloved iron grip. She'd established All Things Beautiful on a shoestring budget at the age of twenty-one and steadily built it into a thriving business in the seven years since. She had a spotless reputation in the community, provided a valuable service for a fair price, and employed two full-time and two part-time workers.

And, apparently, a stoic Pruxnæ with sharp eyes and a sexy grin.

As soon as they'd arrived that morning, Benar had inspected her store from one flower filled end to the other and muttered under his breath in at least two alien languages over, as he'd put it, her pitiful lack of security.

A camera on the back door and above the cash register, deadbolts on the entrances, and an alarm triggered to alert the police in the event of a break in. High tech stuff in Rabun County. Not so much in the rest of the Milky Way, it seemed.

Yasmin hid a grin as she rang up the sale of half a dozen Ice Punch poinsettias for one of her most loyal customers. After the detailed security check, Benar had scrounged her tools and started working on a leaky faucet in the employee bathroom. Next had come repairs to a less than sturdy display table, and after that, he'd repaired a loose board on the back steps, fixed a drawer in the front counter that had never closed well, and scrubbed the floor of one of her flower coolers until it shone like new.

One thing she could say about the ab Mhij men. Hard work didn't scare them a bit.

She handed change and a receipt to old Mrs. Scruggs, accompanied by a sincere smile. "I hope you enjoy these poinsettias, Sally Mae."

"Oh, I will. My house will be the envy of every retired teacher in the county." Mrs. Scruggs adjusted wire-rimmed glasses on her carefully powdered nose and dropped her rounded tones to a bare whisper. "Is that your new fellow I saw working back there, Yasmin?"

Yasmin ducked her head, hiding the slight heat flushing her cheeks on the pretext of sorting receipts in the cash register. Benar wasn't her fellow, though he seemed determined to be in the near future. She just hadn't decided yet if she wanted him the same way. "He's Rachel Hunter's future brother-in-law. Did you meet her fiancé Dyuvad while he was here this past summer?"

"Oh, I did indeed. A sweet boy, good heart, and just as handsome as his brother there." Mrs. Scruggs sniffed delicately and readjusted her glasses. "A sight better than that scalawag Marty Benfield. I taught him in second grade, you know. Always hiding trouble behind that smarmy smile of his."

A story Yasmin had heard often, one she wished she'd listened to before accepting Marty's invitation to lunch that first time. Unfortunately, wishes didn't work that way, but the past was the past. Water under the bridge and the trash with it, as far as she was concerned.

She nodded to one of her full-time workers, pulling Esme away from the display of brightly colored poinsettias she was rearranging. "Let Esme help you get these to your car."

Mrs. Scruggs brightened. "Oh, that would be delightful. Rumor has it Jeremy Darnell is courting Esme's daughter, and her only sixteen!"

And Mrs. Scruggs would love to have the full tale to share at her weekly bridge club, Yasmin guessed. She said her goodbyes to the elderly woman and turned back to her work, smiling in spite of the unpleasant reminder of fiancés past. This was community, people who loved and supported you, people you could count on to bring laughter and cheer into your life even on the darkest day. People you were proud to love in return and call family.

The bell dinged over the front door. Yasmin glanced up and pursed her lips together around a groan. Marty stood in the doorway blocking another customer trying to get in, all five eleven of him. He hitched up chocolate brown slacks under his wool winter coat and beamed at her, flashing a too bright smile. Darn thing could con an Inuit into buying ice.

Old Mrs. Scruggs was right. Marty's smile *was* smarmy.

Yasmin shut the cash register door and scooted around the counter, trying hard to muster a polite smile for her ex-fiancé. She snagged his elbow and pulled him into a quiet corner, away from the new customer and her employees trickling in and out of the main room. "Hey, Marty. Are you looking for flowers for your mother?"

His smile dimmed a watt. "It's Wednesday, time for our weekly lunch date."

"We don't have a weekly lunch date anymore, and haven't since I gave your ring back."

"Aw, come on, Yassy."

She ground her teeth together. Madre de Dios, she hated that nickname, always had, and had asked him not to use it from day one. That should've been her second clue not to date him, right after Mrs. Scruggs' warning.

"We have a lovely selection of poinsettias," she said. "Esme just rearranged them with some from today's shipment. I bet your mother would love to have a few to set out on her staircase."

Marty's smile faded all together. He brushed his stylishly cut dishwater blond hair off his forehead, away from the small vee forming between his sky blue eyes. "You want me to beg? You want me to admit I was wrong to push you about your brother?"

"I want you to quit coming around here and acting like we haven't broken up."

His features melted into a puppy dog plea. "I want you back."

"I'm not taking you back," she said flatly. "Not now, not ever. I thought I'd made that clear."

A warm hand curved around her waist and pulled her against a firm, male side. "There's another delivery man here, beauty."

Relief flooded through her, so swiftly she could've cried. Trust Benar to come to her rescue just when she needed him, exactly the way his brother had been there for Rachel. Yasmin turned a genuine smile on her resident mercenary and stared up into his handsome face. His mouth was curved into a soft smile, but his eyes were flat, cold. She'd ask him about that later. At the moment, she was so grateful for the interruption, she could've kissed him.

"Thanks, Benar," she said. "I'll be right there."

Marty cleared his throat and shot her a questioning look. "Your hired help is getting awfully familiar with you, Yassy."

Benar laughed, that low, husky laugh she was beginning to enjoy a little too much. "I'm not the hired help. I'm her lover."

A muscle ticked in Marty's jaw and his cheeks flushed. "I'm sorry. What?"

Yasmin resisted the impulse to elbow Benar hard in the ribs. Maybe if Marty thought she was seeing someone else, he'd leave her alone. "Benar, this is Marty Benfield, a local banker."

"Yasmin's fiancé," Marty said stiffly.

"Ex-fiancé, and we're not getting back together." She risked draping an arm around Benar's lean waist. He was the one who'd come up with the lover scam. There was no harm in her playing along, was there? "Benar, corazón, could you please start the delivery for me? I'll be right back, I promise."

He stroked a fingertip down the line of her nose and flicked the end. "Anything, beauty."

Yasmin turned and watched him walk away, as a good lover would, and allowed herself a small moment of pleasure in his confident saunter. They sure did put men together well among the Pruxnæ, tall and handsome with very fine rears, at least for the two she knew.

"I see what you're doing," Marty said.

Irritation fluttered through her. God, he was persistent. Just once, she'd like for him to accept what she said at face value. He never had, not in all the years they'd been dating. That should've been clue number three that she was destined for other things.

She turned back to him and eyed him coldly. "What is it you think I'm doing?"

"Trying to make me jealous, and God, Yassy. It's working."

He hooked perfectly manicured hands on his perfectly toned hips, and for the first time, Yasmin saw him for what he really was, a pretentious, narcissistic fake. Not a bad man, no, just a self-centered one, too concerned about his own image and place in the community to truly care about anyone else. She'd spent years catering to his whims, always worried she'd never measure up, and for what? To soothe his ego, to keep a man she'd thought she loved in her life?

And she would've kept right on doing the exact same thing if not for the troubles caused by her brother's old gang the summer past. That made two good things to come out of such hardship, Rachel meeting Dyuvad and Yasmin seeing the light.

She took his hands in hers and held them gently. "Pick out a poinsettia for your mother, on the house. Tell her I'll stop by and visit after the holidays."

"But I—"

"No, Marty. You're always welcome to do business here, but don't come back seeking to renew our relationship."

"Yassy, please."

"My name is Yasmin," she said firmly, and guided him toward the Christmas displays. "Esme will help you when she comes back inside."

With that, she turned and left, ignoring the curious glances from the unknown customer. No more throwing good after bad where the men in her life were concerned. No more settling for second best, no more compromise, and darn tootin', no more smarmy smiles.

She sailed through the employees only door into the back room wearing a grin so big, it hurt her cheeks. Marty had been right about one thing. It was time for lunch. She couldn't think of a better group of people to have it with than the men and women who'd helped her build her pride and joy into a worthwhile enterprise.

And she didn't mind including her erstwhile savior among that number one bit.

CHAPTER FOUR

As SOON AS the sun set behind the rolling hills surrounding the main town, the temperature dropped from balmy to near freezing. Benar gathered the bags of groceries Yasmin had purchased on their way home from her place of business and pulled them out of her vehicle. Snow was coming that evening, she'd said, a big one for the time of year. Word was it would strand local residents in their homes for at least two days, maybe more if ice formed because of it.

Yasmin met him at the door and held it open for him. "Thanks. Sorry. I'll get the rest."

"There is no more." He hefted his load onto the counter beside the sink as Yasmin shut the door and followed him into the kitchen area. "I'll gather firewood while you put this away."

"There's a cord and a half out back, next to the addition."

"Then I'll bring enough in for the night. When was the last time you used the fireplace in your bedroom?"

She paused in the middle of unloading a bag of dairy products. "Last winter? I hardly ever light a fire in there unless the power goes out."

"I'll light one tonight and check that everything works properly."

"I can do that, you know."

"It's man's work."

Her laughter rang out, sweet and honest and bright. "I can't believe your mother allowed you to grow up with such outdated notions. I thought she was a soldier like you before she met your father."

"She was the best. Fierce, determined, loyal."

He eased behind Yasmin, trapping her between his larger body and the counter. The faint aroma of hothouse flowers mingling with the light scent of her soap drifted to him. Unable to resist the temptation, he brushed his face against the side of her neck and breathed her in. Soon, he'd have her under him, free of clothing and inhibitions, and he could taste her, pleasure her, bring her to life in a way no other man could.

Including that winyu's ass Marty Benfield.

"And yet," Yasmin said, "she managed to rear at least two men who think women aren't capable of taking care of themselves."

He ignored the wry humor underscoring her words and aligned his body more firmly with hers. "Hush, woman, and get to work. I'm hungry as a bear."

"I see you spent a little too much time with Ernest today."

"Your hired man is very wise. He advised me to snatch you up before some other whippersnapper came along and stole you out from under my nose."

"He did not!"

"By Wode, I swear it."

The elderly delivery man had also instructed Benar on the reason for all the holiday fuss, and had slipped him a sprig of mistletoe with a saucy wink of one rheumy eye. "For when the weather turns bad," Ernest had said. "Catch her under it and see if that doesn't help you talk her into a smooch or two."

The plant was now tucked safely into Benar's jacket, awaiting just such an opportunity. He was confident he could talk Yasmin into a kiss well before the weather turned, but it didn't hurt to have a backup plan.

She elbowed his stomach lightly. "Don't get any ideas. I'm allowing you a little leeway today because you stepped in and helped me get rid of Marty, but don't think it gives you any hold over me."

He deliberately bumped his hips into her firm ass. He was already holding her and had no intention of letting her go, not until he'd gotten what he wanted from her. "Does leeway include a kiss?"

"It most certainly does not," she said tartly. "And if you want to eat, the leeway needs to end now so I can start supper."

That was a threat his stomach insisted he concede to. He smacked a kiss to the side of her neck, enjoyed the soft intake of her breath and the stillness she fell into. There was passion there, hidden under the all-business façade she maintained. A cautious man coaxed the passion into the open with gentle words and a firm touch. A wise man knew when to touch and when to bide his time.

Benar was both, when he needed to be.

The roll of tires against gravel gradually grew louder outside. Yasmin elbowed him again and wiggled away from the shelter of his body. "That's probably carolers, and here I am with nothing to offer them."

"Carolers?"

"People singing holiday songs to each other. It could be the posadas, though. A re-enactment of Mary and Joseph's journey to find shelter the night Jesus was born?" She shook her head, hurried to the window overlooking the driveway, and peered around the curtain through the frost lined window. "No one told me my home was an inn stop. I don't even have a candle lit or a song prepared..."

"Yasmin," he said. "Be calm."

She inhaled deeply and placed a hand on her flat stomach. "Sorry. My grandparents brought the tradition here when they immigrated from Mexico and my parents have played a huge role in keeping it alive."

"And now you must carry on their work." He leaned against the counter, facing her, and shrugged. "I understand traditions. My people have many."

"Oh, I've heard all about your traditions, Benar Q'Mhel. Don't think you're going to cart me off against my will for some crazy marriage ceremony halfway across the galaxy."

He grinned. "Wouldn't think of it."

"Sure you wouldn't, what with your he-man, I'm the boss ways." She breathed deeply again as loud footsteps banged against the front porch's wooden steps. "Here we go."

A firm rap landed on the front door. Yasmin opened it wide, and went deathly still. "Oh."

The man on the other side was her height, no more, with swarthy skin and a wide, flat nose. He was dressed in a long, black woolen coat and held a large basket filled with fruits in his gloved hands. "¡Feliz Navidad!"

Yasmin swung the door nearly closed and stationed herself behind the gap. "Valentin, what a surprise. You'll pardon me if I don't ask you in."

Her voice shook and her hand trembled on the door's edge. Benar frowned. When confronted by irritated customers and a man claiming to be her fiancé, Yasmin smiled and placated and soothed without allowing anyone to know she was maneuvering them into doing as she wished.

With this stranger, she took a defensive stance, protecting herself from...what? Was this the man responsible for the trouble she'd had lately? Was this her enemy, bearing gifts and a friendly smile?

Benar pushed away from the counter and strode across the room. Beyond the porch, three men ranged across the stairs, each with his coat tucked behind a weapon holstered at his hip. Benar nudged Yasmin out of the doorway and behind himself, where he could protect her if her visitor and his coterie proved as deadly as they looked.

Valentin black eyes flicked from Yasmin to Benar and back again. "Yasmin, chica. Those troubles are behind us now."

She huffed out a humorless laugh. "Sure they are."

"Truly. You're a cherished member of our family."

"You're mistaking me for my brother, who is now in prison serving time for a crime he committed because of you."

"Not me, chica."

"Then someone like you." She shivered and wrapped her arms across her chest under her breasts. "Please leave."

"Of course." Valentin stepped back and placed the basket on Yasmin's doormat. When he rose to his full height, he met Benar's gaze steadily. "A rumor has reached me, that the beloved sister of my brother is suffering. Is this true?"

Benar grunted. By Wode, he would never admit that to the man who might have directed someone to cause that suffering. "Yasmin asked you to leave."

Valentin studied Benar for a long time, as one soldier does another, and finally nodded. "You know how to reach me if you need my support. Feliz Navidad, Yasmin."

She turned her face away and hunched her shoulders around her ears, and Benar's patience snapped under the thrust of righteous fury. He shut the door on the strangers and locked it. Them, he'd handle later. If he discovered that Valentin was behind Yasmin's troubles, he'd repay that suffering tenfold, in the manner of his mother's people. The Q had their own way of dealing with the galaxy's trash and it wasn't pretty.

Let it be so here as it was there.

He wrapped his arms around Yasmin and pulled her against his chest, comforting her with his strength. "One word from you and they're all dead."

Her startled laugh feathered through his thin turtleneck and hit his skin, warming him. "It's nothing, Benar."

"Nothing leaves you shaky and pale?"

"I'm ok. Really."

"You'll be ok, woman, when I say you're ok." He tucked her head under his chin and rubbed her back, each stroke long and slow and soothing. "Trust me to take care of you."

"I can take care of myself."

"Then trust me to take care of what's bothering you. That's why I'm here."

"I know," she said softly. "I never thanked you for traveling here. I never..."

Her words trailed off, interrupted by a muted sob. Benar's heart twisted in his chest. Yasmin was stronger than he'd thought, so much stronger than she appeared, but even a strong woman had a breaking point.

Even a strong woman needed to be held sometimes.

He kissed her temple and whispered comfort words to her in

every language he'd ever learned, and held her through the quiet storm of worry she cried into his embrace.

YASMIN COOKED SUPPER with her eyes averted away from Benar bringing in firewood and setting up a security system in and around her home. What had possessed her to break down like that and cry all over him? Him, a near stranger who was here helping her out of the goodness of his heart.

He'd had to change into a dry shirt before starting his chores.

She hid a cringe behind one hand, mortified to the bone. He must think her as weak as a kitten after that display.

Not that she cared.

She poked the meat filling simmering in a saucepan on her stove, frowning. That's right. She *didn't* care about a stranger seeing her cry, and that's all Benar was. A really hot stranger, sure, but a stranger nonetheless, so what was she so embarrassed about? He'd only be here for a few days, God willing, and then he'd be gone, probably without giving her and her tiny little problems another thought.

Strong hands cupped her upper arms and guided her back into a warm, male body. "That smells good. What is it?"

"Ground beef, onions, and spices," she said. "We're having burritos."

"I like them already."

She twisted halfway around and met his gaze. "You don't even know what that is."

"I'll learn, just as you will." He slid a fingertip along her lower lip, slow and feather light. "We'll fit together so well."

The softly spoken words shivered down her spine, dragging heat with them, and she shuddered, all too aware of the press of his maleness against her hip, the solid width of his chest, the hard muscles of his arms and thighs. He was so unapologetically male, so beautifully real.

And if she didn't know better, she'd swear he was flirting with her.

28

He tapped her lip gently. "I have something to show you after we eat."

"What?"

"A surprise."

He dipped his head and touched his mouth to the pulse beating in her neck, and lingered there, sliding his tongue over her skin as he sucked lightly. Desire throbbed through her and her head fell back against his shoulder. She should stop him, she really should. A chaste woman never allowed a man to touch her so boldly on such short acquaintance. The least she could do was protest or pull away or do *something* to demonstrate that he couldn't do whatever he wanted to her, whenever he struck a notion to.

All her internal arguments fell on weak limbs and eager nerves. Her eyelids fluttered shut as Benar shifted her around in his hold. He kissed the other side of her neck, flicking his tongue along her heated skin. She melted in his embrace and a soft moan escaped her throat. Oh, he was good, so good. Maybe it wouldn't hurt to enjoy his touch for a little while longer.

He trailed his mouth along her jaw and nipped her earlobe. "That's it, beauty. Yield to me."

The words splashed down around her, chilling her as effectively as snow down the back of her shirt. Why, that no good mercenary-soldier was trying to seduce her. Her! And she'd almost let him get away with it, too, out of her own stupid neediness.

She stiffened and pulled away, then turned back to her cooking. "This should be ready in about twenty minutes."

"Yasmin..."

"Go wash up. Guest or no, you'll have clean hands at my table."

He laughed and scraped his teeth along the side of her neck, raising delicious goose bumps along her skin, but he went, taking his solid warmth and wicked touch with him.

As soon as he was out of sight, Yasmin slumped against the counter next to the stove. She really needed to get out more, didn't she, if all it took to arouse her was a sexy man with a willingness to explore her body. She'd be good from now on, avoiding his touch, keeping a firm distance, and if that didn't work, she'd turn her mother's Spanish temper on him.

She chuckled under her breath as she cut the stove off and drained the meat. That should do the trick but good, and she'd try it the very next time he made one of his slick, practiced moves.

Later, though, her resolve dimmed. Benar charmed her over a supper of homemade burritos, teasing her out of her shell in that persistent way of his, never giving her an opportunity to close herself off fully.

Finally, she gave in and asked what she'd been dying to know since she'd learned Dyuvad was an extra-terrestrial. "What's it like out there, in the rest of the galaxy?"

Benar laid his fork on his plate and leaned back in his chair, spearing her with midnight blue eyes. "Not as different from Earth as you'd think."

"That doesn't tell me anything."

He shrugged. "Humans are the same wherever you go. Some live in squalor, some in splendor. Most are somewhere in between."

She leaned forward, unable to hide her curiosity. "But what about all your technology? You've mastered interstellar travel and space communication and who knows what else."

"Not everyone has access to that technology," he said gently. "Some eschew advanced technology entirely and cling to a simpler way of life. Is that not true here?"

Her mouth twisted into a frown. "Yes, I suppose it is."

"It's the same out there, among the stars. My mother's culture is highly advanced, technologically. They embrace whatever helps them move forward. My father's people are primarily farmers, using technology only when it suits them."

"And you're a product of both. Have you never been caught between the two?"

"My parents worked hard making sure my brothers and I learned and respected both cultures."

"You have another brother?"

"Styadun, the eldest of us. He is training to become the kafh of Tyansk Province on Abyw."

"Your home world?" At his nod, she said, "And you followed in your mother's footsteps?"

"I have, from the age of seven, when I began training with the Q."

"Seven!" She inhaled a sharp breath. "So young."

"It was a path I chose willingly."

"But seven. It must've been hard to leave your family like that."

"Sometimes, it was difficult to be away from them. Mostly, I was too busy training to miss them." He stood and held his hand out to her, his gaze warm in an otherwise stony expression. "It's time."

She eyed his hand warily, her earlier resolution fresh in her mind. The last time they'd touched, she'd nearly lost herself under the sensations he'd given to her. She wasn't quite ready to lose her senses again, not today, anyway. "Time for what?"

"Time for you to learn firsthand what space is like."

Her eyes flew to his. "Really?"

"Take my hand and see."

That was one offer she simply couldn't refuse. She slid her hand into his and allowed him to tug her upright. "Where are we going?"

"You'll see." He tucked her firmly against his length and murmured a soft, "Exhale."

So she did, emptying her lungs in a short whoosh of air. His arms tightened around her, and then the world disappeared in a kaleidoscope of color.

She woke to gentle taps on her cheek and the low hum of an engine.

"Wake up, beauty," Benar said. "Our time is short."

She blinked her eyes open and sat up, gingerly prodding the dull ache pounding in her temples. The surface beneath her gave way under her hand. It took her a full minute to piece together the information slowly seeping into her fuzzy brain. She was on a bed, narrow and utilitarian, in a Spartan room with institutional gray walls and bland carpeting of some sort. There were no pictures on the walls, no shelving. A low, black cabinet occupied the corner opposite the bed and a sturdy trunk, also black, sat at the foot of the bed.

She didn't recognize any of it.

"Where are we?" she asked. "What happened?"

"We jumped onto my ship."

"I have no idea what that means."

"I'll explain it later, when we're not in a hurry." He smoothed a stray curl away from her face and tucked it behind her ear. "Ready?"

It took her three tries to stand upright without dizziness pulling her down again, and another two to take her first step. Whatever jumping was, it sapped the energy right out of a body.

Benar had pity on her and wrapped a toned arm around her waist, encouraging her in soft murmurs to lean on him, to use his strength.

And she did, only out of necessity. On her own, she would've fallen. With Benar helping her, she managed to stagger out of the sparsely decorated bedroom down a long corridor into a ruthlessly efficient room with an oddly shaped instrument panel on the far end.

He eased her into a chair near the middle of the room and situated himself with feet widespread in front of the panel on a circle carved into the floor. The wall in front of him lit up as Earth shimmered into view, and her headache fled. She was really in space, her, a small town girl from the middle of nowhere. She was in space on a spaceship at a time when most Earthlings only dreamed of traveling between the planets, let alone beyond them.

The wonder of it filled her, lifting her into the kind of awe she'd only ever felt during prayer. On the wall, blue, blue water and massive continents played peekaboo behind wisps of clouds. A storm system covered parts of the Southern Appalachians, blocking the mountain range from sight, but the rest of it was as beautiful as any picture she'd seen of her home from space. More, even. This was firsthand, not a grainy textbook illustration, too tiny to make out the details of mountain peaks and desert flats. And she was fortunate enough to witness it, thanks to the man standing across the room from her.

She stood slowly and walked on unsteady limbs across that room, coming to a stop beside him. "Thank you, Benar."

He draped an arm around her shoulders and pulled her against his side. "You wanted to know what space was like. This is part of it."

"I didn't think it would be like this, so huge and empty and..."

She laughed, a breathless expression of discovery and gratitude, mingling with the joy of knowing something few Earthlings ever would. "You didn't have to bring me here."

"Yes, I did."

He tilted her chin up and leaned down, and slid his lips over hers, sweetly melding their mouths together. A slow flame ignited deep within her and she melted into him, giving to him what he'd shared so freely. His passion, his touch, this sacred part of his life. Hers now, for this moment, in a way that meant so much to him.

He moaned against her mouth and deepened the kiss, flicking his tongue along her parted lips, and she was helpless to deny him. She opened for him, encouraging him to explore her with soft mewls and the eager splay of her fingers along his lean chest. The fire burning in her grew and grew, building under each sweep of his tongue into her mouth, on the firm grip of his hand on her bottom, in the desperate beat of his heart against hers. It consumed her, singeing her resolve into a handful of ashes in the refuge of her mind.

And for the first time in her life, she burned with need for a man so strong, it was sharp and utterly terrifying.

He eased away from her, panting softly, his muscles trembling where they'd always been so steady, and she buried her face against his chest, certain she knew exactly how he felt. Her own limbs were weak, her heart a thready patter behind her sternum, and the greedy lust he'd aroused in her had barely diminished under the lack of his touch.

"Beauty," he murmured. "We have to go now before the storm worsens."

She nodded and clung to him as they exhaled together and the world disappeared, leaving only him as her anchor.

CHAPTER FIVE

THE SENSOR ALARMS vibrated through Benar's wrist, waking him from a deep, dreamless sleep. He took stock automatically. Yasmin was curled up beside him, her head on his shoulder, one leg over his. She'd started the night out on her side of the bed, as she'd put it. As long as she ended up where he wanted her, he didn't care where she began.

The room was cold beyond the chill of the low temperature Yasmin had set the furnace to before bed. He risked raising his head, peering through the preternatural darkness in search of light, and found none. The power must've gone out overnight. Thankfully, the sensors he'd installed around her home were equipped with fully charged, light absorbing nanobatteries.

Something must've tripped them.

He eased out from under Yasmin's comforting weight and rolled off the bed. *Time,* he thought, and grunted when his implant fed it into his mind, showing a time near when Yasmin's stalker had left his gruesome present on her porch the previous day.

Benar groped along the end of the bed for the clothes he'd laid there and yanked them on as he issued silent commands through his implant. An infrared sensor sweep filled his mind, overlaying the darkened room his eyes were slowly adjusting to. A bulky figure was crouched on the front porch on the other side of the main entrance.

And Benar knew exactly what that figure was doing.

He retrieved a night vision eyepiece and fitted it over his left eye, blinking until his eyes and brain coordinated and he could see clearly.

It was one augmentation he'd refused to have his eyes surgically altered for. The technology hadn't been perfected yet, judging by the number of dal whose augmentations malfunctioned in the field or who lost their vision outright.

He called up a live feed of the front porch and studied it. The figure was still there, absorbed in his work. Good. That gave Benar plenty of time to prepare before he stalked his prey.

Yasmin stirred and groaned. He tucked the covers tightly around her shoulders and smoothed her hair back. Her features were tinged an eerie, electric blue through the NVE and her soft breaths were small puffs of pink, swirling out of the sensual curve of her mouth. She'd been so willing earlier when he'd kissed her, so pliable and giving. He'd taken what he'd wanted from nearly the first moment he'd seen his beauty, her passion, her warmth, her will, so much stronger than he'd dared believe.

A pang shot through his heart and it clenched tightly in his chest, one hard throb of need and a faint emotion he thought might be genuine attraction. He shoved it down as he pressed a gentle kiss to her temple and tucked it firmly away. Feelings had no place in a soldier's life. He'd learned that his first week on Q as a child, alone and lonely among a small army of young.

The backdoor's hinges squawked a mild protest as he slipped through it and into the frosty winter air. A hand's breadth of snow had fallen overnight. Fat globs of it floated lazily to the earth. They'd have another hand's breadth by daylight. Travel would be difficult. Yasmin wouldn't be able to get to her store...

He frowned and stared down at the toes of his boots, already coated with a dusting of snow. His discipline had never failed him before. Once he put something out of his mind and focused on the job at hand, it was the only thought he had room for. That sharpened self-control had helped catapult him through the lower ranks into a leadership position as an exalted Q'Mhel, first among his dal. It had earned him the praise of the soldiers above and below him and, most importantly, of his mother, a former Q'Mhel whose legend was whispered in rumors from trainee to soldier to leader.

He'd always envied her position and emulated her drive, and

35

now it failed him, when the woman he wanted was depending on him to protect her.

A scraping sound drifted to him through the thick air, snapping Benar to full attention. The intruder. Whoever it was had to be finished with his work by now. Benar shook off thoughts of his lapse and crept around the side of the cabin, his steps silent in the wet snow. He reached the edge of the wall and eased his head around, sneaking a look at the spot where the figure had been.

The porch was empty, lifeless, and too dark. The power outage had affected more than Yasmin's cabin. The street lamp was out, too, and with it gone, the intruder could move without being spotted by using the pitifully inferior night vision technology available on Earth.

But Benar wasn't from Earth. His equipment had been developed by some of the best minds in the galaxy and field tested by the toughest mercenary-soldiers among the Q.

And he'd barely begun to use its vast array of capabilities.

With a hyper-focused thought, he enabled the NVE's full complement of vision enhancements. The figure popped into focus twenty-two ceg away, moving carefully away from Yasmin's home toward the spot it had disappeared into the previous morning. Benar followed more rapidly, his footsteps sure along the uneven ground.

He closed the distance easily. Eighteen ceg, fifteen. The figure was ahead of him now, fumbling with the door of a rugged vehicle well suited to rough terrain. The harasser was nearly as tall as Benar and wrapped from head to toe in insulating clothing, and had sturdy shoulders and a narrow waist, evident even under his gear. A human male, but who?

Benar dropped low and edged closer, creeping around the back of the vehicle, still eight ceg away.

An animal screeched overhead, a mournful, drawn out *hooo*. The man let out a muffled curse and something small and metallic clicked. Benar ran toward the vehicle, his caution gone. The intruder was in his grasp, so close the heat left behind by his footprints glowed through the NVE's enhancement. Benar could grab him now and stop what was happening to Yasmin before she got hurt in this madman's game. It would all be over, and when it was, he could relax with her, make love to her for days before duty called him back to Q. The vehicle's door opened and banged shut, and the engine roared to life. Benar leapt toward the door, a controlled shove of muscle and sinew. His foot skittered off a loose rock hidden under the snow, throwing him off balance. He teetered and staggered to the side, sliding in the wet slush along the road bed, and nearly landed flat on his ass.

The vehicle rolled forward, steadily gaining momentum as its tires spun, then caught in the wet snow. Benar dropped into a crouch, slowly sweeping his gaze in spiraling circles around the disappearing intruder. Record the scene now. Study the details later, at his leisure.

By Fryw's teat, he'd been so close to ending this, would've if he hadn't allowed thoughts of his woman to distract him.

But she wasn't exactly his woman yet, and maybe that was the problem.

Benar rose slowly, not bothering to brush snow off his clothes, ignoring the wet chill seeping through them into his skin. Yasmin wasn't his woman yet. She hadn't submitted herself to him, but she would. The power was out. Travel along the roadways would be dangerous in her lightweight vehicle. They were likely trapped in her cabin, just the two of them, and he knew exactly how he wanted to spend that time.

He passed his gaze over the vehicle's tracks once more, then turned and jogged toward Yasmin's home. The intruder's mess would have to be cleaned and discarded where she wouldn't discover it. The fires needed stoking. His clothes needed to be laid flat so they'd dry, and then he'd slide back into bed with her and allow her slight heat to warm him, and his to entice her.

Yasmin was awake when Benar finished his early morning chores and eased back into bed with her, stiff from the cold. She captured his numb hands between hers and rubbed softly. In the dim light thrown by the fire he'd freshened, her features were gentle, disheveled, and so lovely, his breath caught in his throat.

"Why were you outside?" she asked.

He settled on the pillow beside her, carefully arranging his chilled limbs away from her much warmer ones. "I was getting firewood."

"You brought in enough last night for a week." She scooted closer and tucked his hands against her stomach, under her firm breasts. "Did he come again? Is that why you were outside?"

"I took care of it."

"Like you took care of it yesterday?"

Her astuteness pleased him, though he wished her to be otherwise on this one matter. He'd taken care of it for her. That should've satisfied her worry. "Isn't that what I'm here for?"

"You're here to help me figure out who's harassing me. I don't expect you to clean up...that."

He jostled her playfully, hoping to elicit a smile. "I'm the man."

"If you feel that way about it, there are plenty of other chores you can do."

He laughed at the wry note in her sleep-scratched voice. "Among the Pruxnæ, the men work and the women direct."

"That's what Dyuvad said. I never believed him." Her eyelids fluttered closed on a dainty yawn, half stifled. "I should go ahead and get up. Alarm's going off soon. Work."

"No work today, beauty. The roads are closed. There's no power."

He tugged his hands out of her loosened grip and wrapped himself around her. Damn his cold limbs. He needed her now, not when they thawed out.

She mumbled softly and relaxed into him, and her breaths evened out, puffing gently against his bare chest. A man could do worse than a woman who insisted on taking care of herself. Much, much worse, he decided, and drifted into sleep.

BENAR NAILED MISTLETOE to the top of the doorway leading into the hallway from the cabin's main room. Yasmin was getting ready for the day in her bedroom, safely ignorant of the mischief Ernest had prodded him into. That morning, she'd awakened wrapped so intimately around him, he'd missed the feel of her limbs against his as soon as she'd stammered an apology and slid out of bed, away from him.

He'd watched her walk into the bathroom on long, slender legs, her taut ass flexing gently under the silky underwear she'd worn to bed, and his body had hardened as swiftly as a cutter knotting through space-time. He'd touched himself, imagining what she would be like under him. How wet her pussy would be, how tight. The way she'd moan against his shoulder when he made her come, if she'd dig her meticulously groomed nails into his skin and arch into his thrusts.

Blood throbbed into his cock with every heartbeat, thickening it into a painfully hard erection. He rapped his forehead against the doorframe. How in just two short days had he gone from thinking about taking Yasmin as a lover to needing her so badly he ached? And Earth days, at that. No woman had ever had that kind of power over him.

By Fryw, he really didn't want to let one have it now.

He stepped off the two-step ladder he'd found tucked into a corner of the guest room and folded it. Yasmin chose that exact moment to open her bedroom door at the opposite end of the hallway. They stared at each other blankly, two adults sharing space in the tiny cabin with nothing to distract them from the attraction pinging between them.

Yasmin lifted her chin and met his gaze evenly. "You found the lanterns."

"In the attic, exactly where you directed me."

"Thank you." She rubbed her palms together, dropped her hands to her side. Her mouth tightened into a firm line, turned down at one corner. "Do you mind cereal and boxed milk for breakfast?"

"We can jump to my ship and eat."

"No, I really need to get to work."

He set the ladder against the wall and pinned Yasmin with a stare inherited from his mother, cold, authoritative, and uncompromising. "The roads are impassable."

"I have to try—"

"We stay here," he said flatly.

"I have the strangest urge to say, 'You're not the boss of me, neener, neener, neener.' " She marched down the hallway and squeezed past him, carefully avoiding touching him. Her eyes were downcast, shuttering her expression. She put her back to him as she gathered boxes out of the cupboards. "I'll get the generator going so we can at least have water and minimal power."

"I'll do it."

"No, I've got it."

"It's what I'm here for."

She slammed a box onto the counter and whirled toward him, dark eyes flashing fire. "I'm not a child, Benar. I've been taking care of myself for a long time, and I certainly don't need an arrogant, overbearing *alien* telling me what to do."

"I'm not telling you what to do. I'm offering to help you."

"Offer!" she sputtered. "What offer? You swagger in here like you own the place, own *me*, and start barking orders. You take over my home, interfere with my business, force yourself on me."

Raw anger flared through him. Dyuvad had asked him to come here and help her, and she'd needed him to. He was protecting her from an unknown menace, exactly as he was supposed to, and she accused him of forcing himself on her?

He reined his temper in, crushing it under the cold iron of his will. He hadn't shown her a tenth of his swagger, as she'd put it. By Fryw, it was time he did.

CHAPTER SIX

YASMIN BRACED HERSELF against the kitchen counter and lifted her chin, staring Benar down with all the defiance of a mountain bred woman. He could keep his help, by golly, it and his sexy accent, too. She was sick to death of men running roughshod over her heart. Her brother Juan and all the trouble he'd brought into her life, Marty with his holier than thou belief in his own superiority, and now Benar, who thought she was a child.

When would a man ever see her as a woman, an equal, and not an object to be used for his own ends?

Benar's expression was the same one he'd worn the first time she'd met him, glacial, hard as stone, and twice as unyielding. He was stock still, a coiled snake waiting to strike, and it occurred to her then that he could cross the space between them faster than she could react. He could be on her in a heartbeat, if he wanted, and there was nothing she could do to stop him.

The knowledge shivered through her on an unwelcome burst of heat, shooting straight into the secret place between her thighs. His agile speed and strength had attracted her from the first. What woman wouldn't want a man whose body and mind were as deadly as the weapons he carried? A soldier, a protector.

A lover.

Desire flamed through her, warring with her anger, and her hands trembled, to touch him, to lash out at him. She clenched them into tight fists against her thighs, staggered by the conflicting emotions

41

roiling through her. Want, need, irritation, a wad of hurt wound around her heart, throbbing painfully in her chest. Why couldn't he simply accept her the way she was? Why did he have to mow her down as if she were his enemy?

His eyes slid down her stiff form, a slow perusal, piercing through to her very core. "I force myself on you."

The simple statement held a dangerous edge, slicing through her rancor, and she winced. She'd said that, hadn't she? And it wasn't true, not exactly. He'd ordered her around, forced her to accept his presence in her bed, but he hadn't forced himself on her. He hadn't hurt her like that.

She opened her mouth to amend the statement and closed it without uttering a sound. Nothing she said would make up for that whopper, but darned if she'd apologize. Benar had trampled all over her, hadn't he? And she'd let him, exactly like the weak little kitten he thought her to be. So no regrets, no sorries, no apologies, not from her mouth.

She lifted her chin an inch higher. Let him figure it out for himself, damn him. Let him stew in her words the way she'd been stewing in his actions, and suffer for it.

In the blink of an eye, he leapt across the room and pinned her against the counter, pressing her into the edge with the weight of his lean hips. His hands caught her wrists, holding them firmly to her sides, and his fingers dug into her skin through her shirtsleeves. He loomed over her, his face harsh in the dim light thrown by the camp lantern sitting on the counter, so much bigger than her in every way, from his height to his muscles to the sheer force of his will.

So much bigger, so much *more*. His erection pressed into her stomach. Its rigid length startled her, stoking the heat raging through her until her anger was forgotten in the thrill of his touch.

"If I were searching for a mate," he said, his voice low and edgy and so thick, she could barely understand him. "You would be on my ship, chained to my bed. You would be under me, submitting yourself to my desire. I would know what it feels like to sink into your wet heat, to fuck you so hard and long, you scream from the pleasure I give you."

Her pussy clenched on a wave of heat and she sucked in a shaky breath. "Benar—"

"Hush, woman," he gritted out. "The only thing saving you from that fate is the promise I made to my brother. For him, I cling to patience, but only for him. For you, I burn."

He released her hands and skimmed them up her arms, a little rough. His fingers caught on her shirt, pulling her sleeves up, then tangled in her hair, capturing her as surely as his words.

"Benar," she said, his name a whisper of desperate need.

"Mine," he said, and claimed her mouth, crushing the last of her resistance under the practiced skill of his kiss. He drove the fire scorching her higher with every grind of his lips against hers, with every flick of his tongue into her mouth, with each thrust of his hips against her stomach. It was madness and awe, like flying on the back of an eagle, aware of the world stretched so far below, not caring how much it would hurt to fall.

She gripped his waist, greedy to know him now, right now in the moment they shared. His kiss was by turns rough and tender, raw and giving. Deep inside, an amorphous emotion kindled, expanding into her chest, engulfing her sex and her limbs, and her mind tumbled into it, only half aware of the descent into an unknown rightness that moved her, claimed her. Her hands trembled at his waist and her heart stuttered. What was he doing to her? How could a kiss, even one as untamed as Benar's, strike such a resounding chord within her?

As if in his arms was exactly where she belonged.

His hands skimmed down her arms again, far more gently, and he fumbled with the fastening of her jeans. He tore his mouth away from hers and buried his face in her throat, exhaling quick breaths into her skin. "Ingin kryw medgel, Yasmin. Arvl bir, lw medgel."

She shook her head, confused by the guttural words. "What..? I, um. English?"

"Off," he said, and it was all she needed. She brushed his hands away from the waistband of her jeans and flicked the button open, not hesitating a single moment to obey the harsh demand. She needed his hands on her, anywhere on her, needed him to quench the passion he'd strummed so effortlessly.

As soon as her jeans were open, he delved into her panties and slid his fingers along her clit in quick circles. Pleasure sparked through her, and she gasped and clutched his waist. Her hips caught his rhythm, rotating into his touch, and he laughed softly and bit her throat, scoring her skin lightly with his sharp, white teeth.

"Let go, beauty," he said. "Come for me."

Her head fell back, inviting him to bite her harder, more, and she sagged against the counter, consumed by the passion rising sharply in her blood, boiling away any reason she might have to stop him. "Benar," she said, a soft, gasping plea for something he held just beyond her reach. "I... Please."

He quickened his fingers against the sensitive nub of her sex and *mmmd* against her skin, and the elusive sharpened into crystal clear ecstasy. She cried out as her pussy clenched and throbbed through a heart-pounding orgasm, shaking her to her core over and over again under his sure touch. She rode the wave of pleasure clinging to him, her anchor, and at last it faded and ebbed, and she found herself again, a lone woman intimately entangled with a man she barely knew.

Shame flooded her cheeks, washing away the last remnant of passion pulsing within her. "Benar, look—"

"Hush, woman." He slid his hand farther into her jeans and slipped a single finger into her pussy. "Tight."

She cringed and turned her face away from him, resting her cheek on his shoulder. Too late to tell him she was one short hop away from being a virgin. He probably thought she was some kind of slut, after the way she'd acted, and who would blame him? No telling what he'd want from her now.

And she wouldn't be able to resist him, not for long anyway, not after what he'd done to her. Already, her blood hummed and pinged, and a steady ache built with every slow stroke of his finger into her core.

Shameless hussy, Rachel would say. Yasmin bit back a humorless laugh. She'd never held the title before, but if she had to be labeled with it, at least she'd gone all out earning it. Rachel would be thrilled, the traitor, but what were friends for?

Benar withdrew his hand one agonizing inch at a time, caressing her gently, and eased away from her. "Get dressed."

She nodded once, a jerky tilt of her head, and tugged her panties into place, pulled her jeans up, fastened them. "We need to talk."

"No more talk, woman." He pressed a soft kiss to her mouth, lingering sweetly for a long moment, then touched his forehead to hers. "Tonight."

The single word fell into the slight space between them, a solemn promise of things to come. Benar backed away from her, his expression unchanged, his midnight blue eyes brilliant. His erection jutted against his pants, plainly evident through the thick material. Yasmin kept her eyes firmly on his until he turned and strode away. The last word he'd spoken echoed in her mind, *tonight, tonight, tonight,* eliciting a shiver of emotion. For the life of her, she couldn't define that emotion, whether it was dread or excitement.

One thing was certain. She'd think about what he'd done to her during the long, winter day ahead, and not a single thing besides.

THE FROSTY AIR chilled Benar through and through. He embraced it, grateful for the cold dimming the wild need thrumming in his veins.

Yasmin had yielded to him, let him touch her. The beauty of her silken heat clung to him, inciting his imagination, prodding the yearning he held to have her, to take her, to claim her as a man does a woman he desires, fiercely and without mercy for her tender sensibilities.

Tonight.

He hunched down in front of Yasmin's generator, stretching taut muscles, and requested a breakdown from his ship. A tick later, the schematics flooded into his mind, exploded into separate components, probable operating instructions included.

Some days, technology was great. This was one of them. Otherwise, he'd have to go back in the house and ask Yasmin, and would renege on his promise to wait until later before ravishing her.

Slowly, thoroughly, and for a very long time.

He shifted his stance as he examined the generator for wear and tear, and his breeches tightened around his painfully hard erection. Kraden thing refused to ease, in spite of the cold, in spite of the rigid control he exerted over his body. A first for him. His mother would frown on the lapse in his discipline. His brothers would tease him relentlessly about the woman, but his father? He would begin preparing to receive a new daughter into his family.

Yasmin would like the stalwart kafh of Tyansk Province.

Benar frowned at the generator. Why were his thoughts wandering along that path? Yes, he'd threatened her with abduction in the way of the Pruxnæ, but she was a temporary liaison, a lover to fit his mood and the moment at hand. Nothing more.

Which made his preoccupation with her all the more astounding. Yasmin had a life here, a business, a loyal group of friends and family. She would never gladly submit to being stolen from her home, and Earth was too far from the center of civilized space for him to travel here frequently between assignments. A relationship would never work.

And yet, he yearned.

He cranked the generator, listened carefully to the roar of seldom used machinery. It humped along, merrily jittering through slight sputters and stalls, then caught and ran smoothly. The stench of gasoline and mechanical parts filled the air.

Benar snuffled the odor out of his sinuses as he stood. There was plenty of other work here to occupy his time and distract him from the woman waiting inside for him. His ship's AI was dissecting the video from earlier that morning and searching through Earth's databases for matches to Yasmin's stalker and his vehicle. Until it finished its analysis, Benar could scour the property for other clues, check the surveillance cameras he'd set up, set a nice, little trap for the winyu's ass harassing his woman.

He nearly winced at the gut-led description. She wasn't his woman yet. Tonight, though. Tonight she would yield to him fully. She'd open to him exactly as he wanted her to, and he'd sink into her one agonizingly slow inch at a time, loving her as a woman should be.

He left the generator to do its work and set out for his own, a part of his mind lingering on exactly how he could coax Yasmin into touching him as he wished her to.

THE POWER FLICKERED on and off all morning, finally resuming full functionality around ten. Yasmin cut the generator off not long after and threw herself into scrubbing her house clean from top to bottom. The roar of plows clearing Warwoman Road through the gently falling snow kept her company.

Benar didn't. He'd disappeared into the cold after bringing her to climax against her own kitchen counter. She hadn't heard a peep from him since.

And she wasn't worried, not one bit. He was a grown man, after all, a trained soldier reared on a snow world. He could handle himself just fine without her thoughts straying to him.

So she called her employees on her cell phone as soon she got a strong enough signal. The weather would clear overnight. Snow would begin to melt as the temperatures steadily rose into a more normal zone for the time of year. Ice would form at night on the roads, but almost everyone would be able to come in to work within a day or so, God willing.

Ernest lived in town near the shop and promised to check on it and the flowers, but she needed to go in herself. Maybe if the roads stayed clear, she could sneak out this afternoon.

Dread caressed her spine, tightening her muscles. She sucked in a hard breath and leaned her forehead on the broom, pausing in the act of sweeping up dead pine needles from around the base of the Christmas tree. When had the simple act of leaving her home become a frightening ordeal?

She swiped a shaky hand across her forehead and snorted out a laugh. Her father had once called her his fearless warrior princess, unafraid of the world and what it held for her. He'd encouraged her in his own quiet way to buck tradition and strike out on her own, in ways her mother never had. Would that he were here to counsel her, to remind her that she was made of sterner stuff.

If her parents weren't on an extended vacation in Mexico visiting distant family, she'd call him. But there was no need to bother him about the problems she'd been having. Benar was here, protecting her, hiding the evidence so she wouldn't walk into it unexpectedly.

At least, she thought he was still here, somewhere.

She shook the thought off along with the dread and attacked the floor. The day wore steadily on as the sun burned overhead on its short, winter journey across the cloud spattered sky. She ate a light lunch alone, turned her attention to rearranging the pantry, and started supper, a hearty beef stew with homemade oatmeal yeast rolls. The snow petered out and ceased its fall to earth.

And still, Benar remained outside.

His absence raised a ruckus of emotions within her after what he'd done to her that morning, and the promise of more to come he'd left hanging in the air. Irritation that she'd given in. Arousal, surprisingly welcome. And finally worry. What was taking him so long? Where had he gone off to that he couldn't even come in to warm up and eat?

She put the rolls in as the sun dimmed behind the stark hills surrounding her home. The backdoor squeaked open, soft footsteps rang out, and relief overwhelmed the turmoil inside her. He was back. He was safe.

And the night was nearly upon them.

She exhaled a whispered sigh and pressed a hand against her stomach, calming the nerves jumping there. If she asked him to, Benar would leave her be, she just knew it. The question was, did she want him to? Was she ready to have sex with a near stranger? Was she ready to make Benar a part of her life that way?

Certainty settled on her, as quickly as relief had. Yes, she was. She wanted his touch, needed it to engulf her, and she wanted to touch him in return, to pleasure him as he'd pleasured her that morning.

Something she'd never done before.

It should be special, then, this time with him, and so, that's what it would be. Her mind raced through one idea after another, lighting, music, possibilities. The bathroom door opened and closed, the

48

shower started, and Yasmin smiled. Benar would need at least fifteen minutes to clean up, plenty of time for the rolls to finish cooking and her to set the stage.

And when he came out, she'd be all his, exactly the way he wanted her to be.

CHAPTER SEVEN

THE SHOWER CUT OFF just as Yasmin settled herself on the foot of her bed. She folded her hands primly together in her lap and breathed through the nerves ricocheting around in her stomach. Everything was ready. The stew was warming on the stove, the stage was set in the living room. The only thing missing now was Benar.

On cue, the bathroom door opened and he stepped out, his long body completely nude, his head bowed under the towel he held in one hand, drying his black hair. Water dotted his chest, clinging to the fine dusting of hair covering it. Hard muscles flexed as he walked forward, and his sex hung heavily between lean, powerful thighs. He was a living, breathing sculpture, chiseled flesh and blood, and breathtakingly beautiful, not in spite of his scars, but because of them. Benar had lived. He'd experienced. He was no soft-fleshed desk jockey putting in time between golf games and business deals. He was real and solid, and for tonight, he was hers.

She inhaled one last breath, shoved her nerves away, and stood. Time to begin.

Benar glanced up, one eyebrow arched, and pulled the towel away from his hair. "Something smells good."

"Beef stew and oatmeal rolls. Have you eaten?"

"Rations."

Dismay twisted in her stomach along with the last of her lingering nerves. He needed food, but what if she lost her nerve before he finished eating and couldn't follow through on her carefully laid plans?

His midnight blue eyes raked down her body and up again, and he met her gaze steadily, only a hint of a smile curving his sensual mouth. "Nervous?"

"Me, nervous? No."

She huffed out a breath at the bald-faced lie. He must think her the biggest fool on the planet and as naïve as a school-aged girl. So be it. Her path was set and his with it, had been since the moment he'd stepped foot on her front porch. As long as he wanted her, what he thought of her didn't matter anymore.

She held out a hand to him, and was surprised when he dropped the towel onto the floor and grasped her fingers in his without hesitation. His hand was warm and slightly damp, and gentle on her fingers. She threaded hers through his, grateful for the small connection. "Supper's ready if you're hungry."

His smile widened into a knowing grin and he shook his head slowly, barely stirring the wet strands of hair brushing his strong shoulders. "Later, beauty."

"Ok, then."

She tightened her hold on him and tugged, leading him out of her bedroom and down the hallway, facing him so she could watch the glow in his eyes deepen and his sex harden into arousal with each of his whisper soft steps along the floor. She stopped under the mistletoe, and laughed when he pulled her into his arms and nuzzled his face along her throat.

"I like this tradition," he said, his voice muffled and a little hoarse. "Maybe I'll bring mistletoe back to Abyw and introduce the kissing custom to my people."

"You haven't kissed me yet."

"Patience, beauty."

His lips grazed her pulse, as gentle and light as a feather. It didn't matter. His touch shot heat through her, striking lightning in her veins. She shuddered and cupped his narrow hips with hands gone shaky. Such a simple kiss to arouse such fierce need. Was it any wonder she wanted him as she did?

He nipped her skin, and she sucked her lower lip into her

mouth, stifling a gasp. "I'd very much like to kiss you now."

"In a tick," he murmured.

"Why do you always kiss me there first?"

"Among my mother's people, the Q—"

"Star Trek?"

He stilled for a moment, then laughed softly against her skin and eased away from her, meeting her gaze. "No, not Star Trek. My mother grew up on a planet known by others as Q. Only those who are part of the culture know its true name."

"Oh."

"The Q are soldiers, trained from birth to fight and win. Trust is difficult, even among lovers."

"That's a hard way to live"

"Yes. Over time, the Q developed customs to heighten trust. Tattoos here and here." He brushed a fingertip over the pulse points at the top of her throat. "Using ink linked to the wearer's emotions, so a lover always knows where he stands with his mate, especially when he kisses her there. The tattoos change color and reveal everything. Her love, her desire, her passion."

Her eyes widened and she blinked at him. "I'm not getting a tattoo for you."

He grinned and tugged her against him, bumping their lower bodies together. "It's for those wanting a permanent mate."

Disappointment curled through the heat, dampening it, and she rocked onto her heels. He didn't want her as a mate. Which was good, of course. It was too soon. They barely knew each other. Plus, she lived on Earth, and he lived somewhere else in the galaxy, on a planet whose name was only known by its own population. It would never work, this thing between them, no matter how brightly it burned.

At least she knew that going in. At least now her hopes wouldn't soar out of control.

His grin slowly faded. He wrapped a hand around the back of her neck, holding her tightly, tenderly. "Yasmin, beauty. Let me love you now."

"Benar." Her voice broke and wavered, and she closed her eyes, gathering her courage for what she was about to do. Making love to a virtual stranger, a man who only wanted her for a short time. Benar, her protector. She swallowed down her nerves and tried again, forcing her voice to be strong, to be as sure as her heart was that this was the right path to step onto. "I laid out blankets for us in front of the fire. I hope you don't mind."

His gaze held hers, never straying beyond her face. "It's perfect."

"Because we could always go to bed or use the couch or—"

He kissed her, silencing her more effectively than any shushing would have, and she relaxed under the steady pressure of his mouth. Silly goose. He was a man. Men didn't care where they had sex, did they? And he was ready for her. The tip of his erection brushed her stomach through her clothing, teasing her with promises of passion yet to be. She wanted to touch him, needed to learn him in that way, and couldn't quite gather the courage to move her hands away from his lean waist.

He broke the kiss abruptly and touched his forehead to hers. His breaths were sharp, harsh, and as unrestrained as the passion gleaming from his dark eyes. "Undress for me in the firelight."

Her hands tightened on his waist. To be nude in front of him, as he was for her? The idea was strangely exhilarating and terrifying all at once. Slowly, she nodded and eased away from him, one small step backward at a time. His gaze clung to her, rapacious and hard, as titillating as having his fingers caressing her.

The heel of her socked foot hit the edge of the area rug, and she stopped. Here was good, on the verge of the place she'd created for them, lit by the fire in the insert and the lights strung around the Christmas tree. Here was where they'd continue what had begun that morning with his kiss, on a layer of blankets she'd spread out for them on the floor in a home that had never known an overnight male guest outside of her family.

She untucked her turtleneck and drew it over her head in one smooth movement, too afraid to take her time and lose what little nerve she'd managed to scrape together. Benar grunted, encouragement or approval, she couldn't tell. She fumbled with the waistband of her jeans. Unfastened them, shoved them down, stepped out of them, and stood trembling before him in a serviceable pale yellow bra and matching panties.

Darn it, she should've changed into something sexier for him.

Benar strode toward her, slowly, as gracefully as a feline stalking his prey. "On your back."

Her legs nearly gave out, would've if he hadn't reached her at just that moment and eased her down onto the blankets. Her bra disappeared, her panties shimmied away under his persistent hands, and he knelt between her spread legs, brushing his fingers in slow circles up her inner thighs.

She shivered and clutched the blanket in tight fists. Already, she burned for him. Wet heat flooded through her, pooling in her nethers, and her pussy throbbed and pulsed. "Benar, please," she whispered, and he laughed and touched a single fingertip to her clit, exactly where she wanted him to.

"You feel so good," he said.

Oh, he had no idea how good she felt, how alive and beautiful he made her feel.

His finger slid down and stroked into her, once, twice, and his hand tightened on her thigh. "You're ready for me."

An embarrassed huff of laughter escaped her. "Yes."

"I wanted to take my time."

He eased his finger out and crawled up her body, grazing his mouth in random spots along her sensitive skin. A nip of her hip, a kiss above her navel, a flick of his tongue along one nipple. She gasped and whimpered and bit her lower lip, stifling the urge to beg. *More, harder, please, oh, please, Benar.*

Something must've escaped, whether she wanted it to or not, some muted plea, some desperate glance. His mouth curved into a smug smile as he settled his weight on her and his erection nudged her core, and he flexed his hips, sliding its tip along her wetness. "I wanted this first time to be sweet and tender, restrained, but you're so wet, beauty, so ready for me. Tell me you want me."

"I do."

"Say the words."

"I—" She swallowed, coating her dry throat, and blurted out her desire. "I want you, Benar. So much."

He pressed forward, sliding his hard length into her core, stretching her almost painfully. "Tight."

And again, the words bottled themselves up, pinned behind her lips.

Because they were, because she had no way of sharing her inexperience, she forced herself to relax under him. He thrust himself in and out of her body, gently penetrating a little more each time. A fine sweat broke out along his skin, gleaming in the firelight, and he murmured to her, strange, guttural words whispered against her temple.

He thrust a final time and seated himself fully on a low groan. "You hold me so well."

She nearly laughed, would've if his hips had stayed still, if he hadn't begun slow, hard thrusts into her, rocking her against the blankets. "It feels good."

"Next time will be easier. Next time—" He sucked in a harsh breath and yanked her arms up over her head, one at a time, pinning her wrists there with one firm hand. "This time, we are wild, like animals mating in the wilderness."

"Benar," she said, so greedy for his touch, she could barely speak. "Please."

"Animals," he ground out and shoved himself into her. "You will come so hard, you shatter, and I will catch your screams with my mouth."

There were no words after that, none she could discern. They were too far gone, lost in the passion rising swiftly around them, an inferno engulfing them in raging desire. His thrusts became swift, short, and hard, and she arched into them, sliding her legs along his, gasping with every burst of pleasure rolling through her. Up and up he drove her, ruthlessly fast, and she went, too overwhelmed by his sensual beauty to resist.

His mouth met hers and devoured her, as wild as the animals he had accused them of being, and he thrust into her a final time and groaned into her mouth, and his release throbbed through her, triggering her own. She moaned and writhed under him, caught in an orgasm so strong, she fractured and reformed, shattering exactly as he'd promised her she would, and in that moment, she became his.

BENAR RESTED his forehead on Yasmin's and struggled to control his heaving breaths, his racing heart, the rugged desire clamoring in him to take her again, harder, faster, forever.

He huffed out a humorless laugh and slid off her, out of her wet heat and onto his side, taking her with him. How his mates would laugh if they could see him now, tamed by a spitting yinga, eagerly domesticated by one good fuck.

He'd been too rough with her. Regret pinged through him, dimming the wild heat still scorching his blood, and he gathered her close, gentling his touch for her. She sighed and settled willingly into his embrace, a small smile on her sweet mouth, and something else pinged through him, something delicious and rich and unfamiliar.

"You have had another," he said gruffly, half afraid to learn how many men she'd accepted, needing to know anyway.

"Once, when I was a teenager. I thought I was in love."

Her soft laugh held the bittersweet memories of long ago youth, and he relaxed, pleased for a reason he couldn't name. "Not that winyu's ass."

She reared back, blinking at him, her lovely face twisted into a confused frown. "What?"

"The ex-fiancé."

"Marty? No, never him."

"You didn't love him?"

"I thought I did, but I could never..." She shook her head, then resettled it on his bicep, sighing into his chest. "It never felt right, so I didn't."

"It felt right with me?"

"That's one way of putting it."

He shook her gently, willing her to satisfy him in this way as well as she'd satisfied him in others. "Tell me straight, woman, before I turn you over my knee."

"You keep threatening me with a spanking. I think you're all bark and no bite."

"A Q'Mhel never threatens, little yinga."

"English, Benar," she said, and her voice was so patient, so even, it stirred that unnamed emotion in him again.

"Yingas are native to Q. They're small at birth, covered in soft, flexible scales, with sharp claws and teeth and the fierce attitude of a woman rebuking her lover."

Her eyes popped open and widened. "Are you teasing me?"

"Yes," he admitted, unashamed of his need to flirt and cajole. She was his woman now, and she deserved to be treasured. And because he could, he tucked a stray strand of hair behind her delicate ear and kissed her softly, reverently, grateful to have discovered her. "We raise them as training beasts, matching them against trainees as the two grow together in skill, age, and size."

"You fought one of these yinga?"

"Many times."

"Is that where you got your scars?"

"A few."

Her fingertips brushed his ribs, tracing the fine white lines marring his skin. "Did one do this?"

He hesitated. Telling her how he'd gotten his scars would open up areas of his life she might not be ready to handle, if she ever could. Too many of his dal mates had lost lovers because of the dangers inherent to their jobs. Benar never had, and he had no wish to lose one now.

She pinched his skin gently, digging her nails into him a fraction. "Tell me."

"My little yinga."

"Now you're stalling."

"Yes."

She levered herself onto an elbow and stared down at him, her expression soft and womanly, except for the determined gleam in her eyes. "No secrets."

"Yinga," he said, a soft tease. "My first mission. I was fresh out of training, barely sixteen years."

She hissed in a breath. "So young."

"Sixteen years on Q," he corrected. "Not quite that here on Earth. We train young, train hard."

She leaned forward and pressed a tender kiss to his mouth. "For the boy who was too young."

"There's no such thing on Q, beauty."

"Yes, there is," she insisted. "Now tell me about this first mission."

"Protection duty, an easy draw," he said, and because he needed her to understand, he added, "We're not thrown to the wolves our first time out."

"I believe you. Who were you protecting?"

"A foreign dignitary from three systems away. He'd received a threat, too vague for his regular security team to pinpoint. They hired my dal—"

"Dal?"

"My unit. I was the youngest, green, cocky."

Her smile flashed, warming him inside and out. "Aren't all teenagers?"

He rolled onto his back and tucked a hand under his head, and grinned back at her. "Yes, but training on Q feeds it to an extreme. I was so sure I could handle any situation."

"Until you were assigned your first duty," she guessed.

"It was supposed to be easy. Go in, protect the dignitary, go home and collect my pay."

"What went wrong?"

"Traitor," he said flatly. "One of the man's people turned on him and leaked information on the security detail to a terrorist group. They targeted me to get to him."

She laid her hand on his stomach and her eyes went wide. "They tried to kill you?"

"Didn't work. I was young, but I wasn't stupid. They overran us at a choke point, tried to herd us into a dead end. I took out three men before the terrorists set off an explosive trying to eliminate me. I woke up in the infirmary on my ship days later with a new scar."

Her fingers skimmed across his body and traced the irregular pattern of scars decorating his ribs. "Your first?"

"Not even close."

"It broke your ribs?"

"Two. Q's medics took the liberty of adding a duro-coating to them while my skin was torn. They never broke again."

"But others have?"

"Not anymore."

"You have this duro-thing on all your bones?"

"Just the ones the medics could get to. Saves on wear and tear in the field."

"What else? Are you..." She shrugged and tapped her fingers against his ribs. "A cyborg or something?"

"Not a cyborg as you understand it, but I have plenty of upgrades." He tapped his left temple. "All trainees have a neural net implanted in their brains as soon as they're selected. It monitors our internals, feeds vitals to medics via our ships so they can tell what's working and what isn't."

"And that's it?"

"No, but it's all I'm talking about today." He slid his free hand up her arm and cupped her nape. "Kiss me."

"I still have questions."

"Later."

She huffed out an exasperated sigh. "You say that now, but when later gets here, you'll give me the run around again."

"Is that what I'm doing?"

"Yes," she said firmly. "Besides. I kind of wanted to..."

Her eyelashes swept down and a faint tinge of pink flooded her cheeks. Benar shifted his head on his hand, aiming for a better look. "You want to touch me."

"I've never touched a man...there."

The idea zipped through him, stronger and faster than lightning, and desire stirred in his manhood. "Put your hand on me."

"No, I—"

"Do you want my hand on your ass?"

"Are you threatening to spank me again?"

"Promising."

"Oh, fine," she said, and draped her hand over his hardening penis. "Happy?"

"Not yet, but I will be soon."

She laughed, bright and free. "So it's true. Even men born on another world only want sex."

"I never said that." He let go of her nape and slid his hand over hers, adjusting her hold, guiding her fingers along the sensitive head of his erection. "Touch me like this."

Her fingers slipped along his glans, shy and hesitant. "You're not circumcised."

The definition of the unfamiliar word flooded into his mind, and he blanched. "That's barbaric."

"Yeah, I guess you'd think so." She stroked her hand over his rigidity from tip to base, and frowned. "What's this?"

He pulled his penis toward his stomach so she could get a better look at the tiny, metal, bar-like device affixed to the base of his penis near his scrotum. "Birth control. It's pinned through the urethra. Kills sperm during ejaculation."

She wrinkled her nose and loosened her hold on him. "And you think circumcision is barbaric."

"This isn't permanent. Pinch the ends together." The corners of her mouth turned down and she slid her hand away from his sex. He snagged it and placed it exactly where he wanted her. "Do as I say, woman."

"Ok, ok," she muttered. "I'll pinch the blasted ends together."

Her fingers fumbled along the base of his penis, brushing against his testicles, eliciting a storm of delicious pleasure. She pinched the ends of the bar together, releasing the internal clamps. It popped away from his skin, and a rush of sensation pulsed through him. He gasped and arched his back, pushing his erection against her hand.

She drew back, taking the device with her, her brows knit above troubled eyes. "Sorry. I didn't know it would hurt."

"It didn't," he rasped. "Straddle me and take me into you."

She dropped the device onto the coffee table shoved against the couch, then straddled his thighs. "But I have so many questions."

"Questions later. Fucking now."

She laughed and scooted forward, dragging her pussy over his erection in a slow, wet glide of erotic heat. "I think I like having you under me at my mercy."

And he liked being there. He guided her hips in a slow grind against his desire, and loved her for a very long time after.

CHAPTER EIGHT

BENAR WOKE with a jolt, filled with a creeping dread. Yasmin was asleep, draped possessively over him. The house was quiet, nothing stirred outside. The alarms keyed to his internal sensors were inactive, untriggered. Everything seemed normal, but his instincts were a quiet, continual scream. Something was wrong, something he couldn't pinpoint.

He focused his thoughts and pushed a query to his ship through his implant. Almost immediately, an all-clear tickled his mind. He had the AI run a sweep anyway, searching beyond the perimeter he'd set up around Yasmin's cabin for any sign of wrong-doing.

Nothing.

Time, he thought, and grunted. Half an hour past when her harasser normally left his gift on her front porch. Last night, the ship's AI had relayed conclusions from the evidence Benar had gathered the previous morning. The vehicle he'd nearly caught had been found by local law enforcement agents, abandoned on the other side of their jurisdiction, well away from Yasmin's home. No fingerprints, no blood, no debris in the interior to suggest the identity of its most recent occupant. It had been stolen from another jurisdiction two days prior. Maybe without this transportation, the intruder was momentarily stymied.

A dead end, but not the only information Benar had gathered. He still had the intruder's height, build, and estimated weight to go on, providing he could narrow down a list of suspects.

Which he hadn't been able to do. Her brother's old gang had

drawn no suspicions during Benar's searches, nor did anyone else associated with her seem to have any reason to harm her. She was nearly universally loved and respected by the people who knew her.

He eased away from Yasmin and out of the warm bed, into the early morning chill permeating the cabin, and yanked on clothing on his way through its rooms. The front porch was empty. A manual search of the area within the perimeter proved equally fruitless. He didn't believe for one tick that the harassment had stopped. It would resume as soon as the intruder found a way to continue his work. That evening, maybe. By the next morning, certainly.

Until then, work of another kind could continue. The roads were mostly clear. Yasmin wanted to return to work, and after the evening she'd given him, he was loathe to refuse her.

He slipped back into the cabin, secured it, added wood to the fires. She was still asleep, her head on his pillow, her lithe body a fragile hump beneath the thick covers topping her bed.

Against reason, desire stirred, and with it, his manhood. Four times, he'd had her last night, and still, the yearning to have her again rested in an aching lump pressed into his heart. And because it did, because something indefinable tied them together now, he undressed and slid under the covers next to her without a single thought more for the lack of a gruesome scene on her porch.

"Benar?" she whispered, her voice softened by sleep and desire.

"Who else would be sneaking into your bed?"

"Just you. Mmm." She slid one leg over his and arched her hips against his stomach. "What are you doing up?"

"Protecting my woman."

"Oh, that again," she said, and the mild humor piqued his own.

"Yes, that again."

He rolled her onto her back and settled himself on top of her, braced above her. His erection slid against her core and he groaned. She was ready for him, hot and wet. Would it always be so between them?

She raked her fingernails lightly down his chest. "Isn't it a little early for sex?"

He laughed and eased into her, gently, slowly, as he'd promised her he would last night, and hadn't been able to, driven by the sheer urgency of their matings. "It's never too early for sex, beauty. Never too late, either."

"Let me guess," she said, smiling. "Any time is the right time."

"Now you understand," he said, and she laughed and wrapped her legs around his waist, and encouraged him with shy whispers and eager caresses.

Later, they showered together in her claw footed bathtub, dressed and ate a light breakfast, and headed to the flower shop, navigating ice spattered roads and sparse, cautious traffic.

As soon as they arrived, Yasmin was off, checking on flowers, calling employees in, answering messages left on the shop's voice mail. Esme came in an hour later, trailed by a grinning Ernest carrying homemade beignets his wife had made, and the workday progressed as it should.

Benar split his time between helping the elderly man load flower arrangements into the shop's van for delivery, making repairs around the shop, and coordinating security with his ship. Around lunch, he noticed a peculiar pattern executed by a young boy on the other side of the road. Stroll up, shelter in a niche at a business across the way, wait a measured amount of time, stroll back down. The actions seemed harmless enough on their own, would've been if the boy hadn't cast furtive glances at Yasmin's shop during his walk, out of a face nearly obscured by a scarf wrapped around his hooded head.

Benar excused himself and left the shop through the back entrance. He triggered a jump via his neural net's link to his ship, and rematerialized half a tick later, directly behind the boy's shelter. The boy stepped out, and Benar leapt forward, subduing the youngster with a well-placed fist to the jaw. The boy crumpled silently under the blow. Benar searched for weapons, slung him over one shoulder, and carried him across the street.

The bell dinged as he entered. Yasmin popped into the doorway separating the business area of the shop from the workspace, and frowned. "What are you doing?"

"Apprehending a suspicious character." He strode past her into the workroom and dropped the boy onto the concrete floor in an empty corner, ignoring Esme's curious stare and Ernest's raised eyebrows. "This one was patrolling outside, surveilling the shop."

"He's just a child," Yasmin said, and brushed Benar out of the way. She knelt in front of the boy and tugged down the scarf, and her frown deepened. "This is a girl."

"Angelina Torres," Esme said cheerfully. "Fernando's eldest. Good girl, that one."

"What was she doing outside in the cold?" Yasmin asked, and shook her head. "Never mind. Oh, look at this bruise. Did you have to hit her, Benar?"

He shrugged. "She's a spy."

"You don't know that."

He snorted. Yes, he did. What else would the girl be doing walking up and down the street? Her age was camouflage, nothing more. Even a small yinga was dangerous. A lack of weapons didn't make this one safe.

Angelina stirred and groaned, and huge blue eyes popped open, a sharp contrast to her olive skin. They skimmed past Yasmin and landed on Benar, and her delicate features snapped into a fierce scowl. "You hit me."

"You were spying."

"Yeah, and?" She wiggled her jaw, palmed it, scowled some more. "Ain't no law against looking a place over."

"There is my law." Benar crouched in front of her, even with Yasmin, and leveled a cold stare on the girl. "Who sent you?"

Her gaze wavered and dropped. "Nobody. I was exercising, is all. Ain't no crime."

"You seem well versed in the law, little one."

"A woman's gotta know her way around it, ain't she? Can't depend on no man."

Yasmin rocked onto her heels, her lips pressed tightly together. "I think some hot cocoa is in order and perhaps a sandwich. Esme, would you call the deli and add a meal to our order?"

"Right on it," Esme said, and bustled out of the room toward the shop's phone.

"I'll get that cocoa," Ernest said, and he disappeared, too, into the tiny employee break room out back.

Benar turned his cold stare on his woman. "You do not reward misdeeds with food."

She waved his stare away, completely unaffected. "Oh, give it a rest, Benar. Angelina meant no harm. Isn't that right?"

Angelina's brilliant blue eyes went round and she nodded solemnly. "I was just minding my own, is all. No harm, no foul."

"Yasmin," he said.

"Benar." Yasmin stood and pulled him up with her, then dragged him to the other side of the room. "Look, I know it's crazy, but I believe her, ok? Plus, I thought, what with you not using, you know."

"No, I don't," he said flatly.

"Birth control," she whispered, so faintly he could scarcely hear her. "When we, you know. And I just... I'm not either and with the chances of *it* happening. Maybe I should practice a little, just in case?"

It took him a tick to piece together what she was saying in her stuttered starts and spurts, and when he did, a fierce ache grew within him. She might become pregnant during their interlude, and rather than rebuffing a possible child, she wanted to prepare for it, against her culture's beliefs, against his. She wanted a child, his child. Theirs.

The yearning to watch her grow round with their child burst into him, staggering him. He wanted that, too, wanted to join his life with hers, wanted to watch over her as she nurtured their young and their family grew.

So much for leaving Yasmin behind when he found her stalker.

He curled his hands around her upper arms and yanked her against him, and kissed her, hard and fast and as greedily as he had the first time their lips had touched. He would give her a child, a boy to carry on his culture, a girl for hers, if Wode so blessed them, and Yasmin would forever after be his.

The rest would sort itself out later, where they would live, their work, all of it. In that tick, he could not have cared less about the rest of the universe.

"Ew, gross," Angelina said. "I'm only eleven, ya know."

Yasmin broke the kiss on an indelicate snort and eased away from him. "She's right. We can talk about this later."

The front doorbell chimed, interrupting Benar's retort, and a familiar and unwelcome voice called a cheerful greeting, answered by Esme's muted response.

Marty Benfield, the winyu's ass, was back.

A cold, calculating smile curved Benar's mouth. "I'll handle that."

Yasmin tilted her head and slowly, a smile lifted her own expression. "I think I'll let you."

"Keep an eye on the spy there," he said. "Put her to work."

"Hey, now," Angelina said, but Yasmin was already nodding and hurrying away, no doubt to practice her parenting skills on Benar's catch.

He strode into the outer room still wearing an emotionless smile, and was pleased when Marty blanched under its frigid chill. Benar stopped beside the front counter, blocking the path into the back rooms, and held his hands at his sides, ready for whatever came his way. "Yasmin is busy."

Marty shoved gloved hands into the pockets of his wool coat. "Not for me, she isn't. Tell her I'm here."

"You misunderstand. Yasmin will always be busy where you're concerned."

Esme ducked her head, hiding a smile, and left, likely to avoid the coming storm.

Blood flushed into Marty's face, mottling the pale, flaccid skin. "Now, see here. She's my fiancée—"

Benar shook his head slowly. "Yasmin is mine. She will never be yours again, Benfield. Come here again and I will brand that into your hide."

"You can't," Marty sputtered, and Benar's patience broke. In a tick, he was on the man, shoving him around and out the door faster than the ass could react. Benar locked the door, flipped the closed sign, and pivoted on the ball of his foot, ignoring the curses Marty slung at the impenetrable barrier.

Yasmin was standing in the space he'd vacated, a curious smile on her face. "I would pay good money to see that."

"See what?"

"You branding Marty's hide." She held her hand out to him, so sweetly, he melted in the face of her beauty. "Ernest is about to pick up lunch. Come clean up."

Benar hitched a thumb over his shoulder. "What about him?"

"If he doesn't leave by the time Ernest gets back, I'm calling the police." She tucked her hand into his and rested her head on his shoulder. "My hero."

"Yes," he said simply, and she laughed and kissed him, and all was right in his world.

THE DAYS FLEW BY faster than Yasmin could keep track. Every night, Benar made love to her, by turns tender and fierce. Every business day, she opened her shop, secure in the knowledge that he was watching over her. Nothing would happen to her while he was around, nothing ever could, and each day that passed only proved it to her over and over again.

Her stalker had apparently given up in the face of his determination, and for that Yasmin would always be grateful.

But it wasn't gratitude that drove her to open her heart to the stalwart warrior. It wasn't gratitude that turned her disinterest into affection and edged into love. It wasn't gratitude that drew her night after night into his embrace, nor did that emotion factor into the secret prayer she whispered as she fell asleep in his arms.

She might be pregnant.

It was a rash hope, one she should strike from her heart before it could take root. A woman of her standing couldn't afford to become pregnant with an illegitimate child, yet there the longing was. Maybe if the possibility were offered by another man, it would be different. She'd never been in a rush to marry Marty so they could start a family, but with Benar, she wanted so much more.

And so she shoved down her worries over what the future would bring, cherished each moment she had with him, and nurtured the possibility of a child deep in her heart of hearts.

On the sly, she ordered a special gift for Benar, rush delivery, and wrapped it, tucking it under the tree with gifts for her family where he wouldn't find it. Not that he was expecting one, she suspected, but he would spend the day with her and she wanted to show him how much he meant to her.

The words hadn't found their way out of her heart yet. It was too soon for declarations of love, even if she could be sure of her emotions.

Benar never revealed his, though he treated her so well, it seemed obvious how he felt.

Most of the time.

At others, she felt certain she was nothing more than one in a long line of many. The thought would've brought her to her knees under the weight of unbearable heartache if not for the rush and hurry of the last few days before Christmas. The shop was slammed with customers needing last minute flower arrangements. Two members of the local community died, necessitating two separate funerals one right after the other, on top of the normal spate of sweetheart vases and get well balloons delivered around the county.

By the time Christmas Eve rolled around, Yasmin was utterly exhausted and so pleased with the way the pre-holiday business had gone, she couldn't quit smiling. Her personal life was still a bit of a mess. They hadn't caught the person leaving nasty-grams on her front porch, though she personally hadn't seen another one. Angelina's mysterious appearance in their lives had also not been solved, though Yasmin suspected that with time, the girl's determined shell would wear down.

And she missed Rachel, missed the girls, missed Fate, too, for that matter. He'd promised to drop by and check on her now and again, but the coot hadn't set foot near her in weeks. It had probably slipped his mind, bless him. She'd check on him tomorrow, take him a hefty plate full of food to tide him over the holiday, along with the present she'd wrapped for him, a brand new book on beekeeping for him to study over the winter.

She swiped the back of her wrist across her forehead, pausing in the act of chopping celery for tomorrow's stuffing. Benar eased up behind her, so silently, she almost missed his approach, and wrapped himself around her, chin on her shoulder, hands splayed wide across her flat stomach.

As if he, too, longed for the child that might be resting there.

Maybe a few of her smiles had another source, though she couldn't quite bring herself to tell him that either.

"The mistletoe is very lonely," he said.

"It can wait until I've finished prepping for tomorrow's meal."

"I can't wait," he muttered. "How much longer?"

She dropped her knife on the cutting board and twisted around, meeting his gaze with her own. "You sound like Angelina."

"Ha. The girl is too impatient for her own good." He nuzzled his face into her throat, licking her pulse. "But I am a Q'Mhel of the first order. Patience has been bred into me since birth, and beaten into me when I forgot the lesson."

She snickered and covered his hands with hers, measuring their strength against her own. "Maybe I need to beat a little into you now."

"You do. Undress and teach me patience, woman."

"Later, I promise."

"Now," he insisted, and captured her mouth with his, kissing her so thoroughly, she completely forgot why they needed to wait.

A hard fist hit the door, startling Yasmin into awareness.

Benar spared not a single glance toward the entrance. "We're not receiving."

"It's Christmas Eve, Benar. It could be family or carolers."

"They'll leave."

"I need to get that."

"You need to—" The fist hit the door again, louder, and Benar cursed under his breath. "Send them on their way."

"As quickly as I can," she promised.

She twisted out of his embrace and hurried toward the door, removing her apron as she walked. The knock came again, more insistently, and she huffed out a small breath. Not family, then, or friends. Only a stranger would be that rude.

She fixed a welcoming smile on her face and threw open the door, freezing in place at her unexpected guest. "Marty. Hey. What are you doing here?"

"It's Christmas Eve, Yassy. We haven't spent one apart since we started dating."

A worm of unease slithered through Yasmin's happiness, puncturing it. She braced her foot behind the door and studied her former fiancé's fixed expression. He was smiling, ever the cheerful loan officer, but his eyes were vacant, focused somewhere behind her.

Focused on Benar.

Yasmin instinctively placed herself between the two men, all too aware of her lover stalking toward her on silent, bare feet, and of Marty's hand moving restlessly in his coat pocket around a bulge too big to be anything other than a weapon. "Go home now, Marty, or I'm calling the police."

"No need, Yassy. This won't take long."

He yanked his hand out of his pocket and aimed a Taser at her. Benar shoved her to the side out of its direct path. The Taser discharged, hitting Benar squarely in the chest as Yasmin's knees cracked into the hardwood floor and she toppled onto her side. His body arched and jittered and collapsed onto the floor, and Marty stood there, pressing the Taser's trigger, that fixed smile never fading as hundreds of volts of electricity pulsed into Benar's twitching form.

"Stop it!" she screamed. "You're killing him!"

Marty jerked toward her, releasing the Taser as he did, and his smile dropped away, leaving his expression wounded. "Don't be mad, Yassy."

She shook her head slowly, pushed herself upright, and staggered to Benar's side, ignoring her bruised knees. He was so pale, so still. She pressed her fingers to his pulse, alarmed by the way it fluttered unsteadily under her fingertips. The Taser's probes were fixed in his chest. She hovered over him, unsure if she should try to remove them, not knowing how to help him.

An ambulance. She had to call an ambulance. The paramedics would know what to do, wouldn't they?

She scrambled upright, aiming for her phone. Hard fingers caught her hair, yanking her to a stop before she took a single step.

She yelped and grabbed the hand holding her in place, attempting to pry it out of her hair.

"It's Christmas Eve, Yassy," Marty said, his voice eerily calm. "I've got a special meal waiting for us at home."

"Let me go, Marty. I'm not coming with you."

"Don't worry, sweetheart. Everything's going to be perfect this year."

He dragged her along behind him through the doorway. Yasmin twisted and screamed, struggling against Marty's brutal grip on her, praying someone would overhear and find Benar before it was too late.

CHAPTER NINE

THE SURFACE beneath Benar was hard, smooth, and impersonally cold. His entire body ached, every muscle, the back of his skull, his chest, and his head was empty of the faint background noise generated by his neural net coordinating his body and mind with his few biomechanical upgrades.

That had only happened twice in his life, once as a trainee on Q when he hadn't ducked fast enough during sparring practice. The other time had been on his first mission, the one he'd shared with Yasmin. Explosions and hard blows could disrupt the net's normal functionality.

And so could an electrical charge.

The first fleeting hint of panic gathered around his heart, squeezing painfully. That winyu's ass was responsible for this. Thank Fryw Yasmin hadn't...

Yasmin!

Benar sat bolt upright, breathing through the screaming agony seizing his body from bone to skin. The lights flickered and slowly brightened, illuminating the interior of his ship's medical bay. A projection of Jira, his dal's medical officer, squatted in the center of the room. Her cerulean hair was knotted into untidy braids sticking out all over her head and she wore a huge, shit-eating grin on her homely face.

"Heard you got stuck by a civvie, B-man."

Benar touched the tips of his index finger and thumb together and flipped his hand over, opening his palm to her. If she could be rude, so could he, and he had a lot of obscene gestures to choose from, half of which meant *fuck you.*

Jira trilled her tongue. "This backwater planet hasn't done a thing for your manners."

"Fuck manners. My woman is in danger."

She rocked back on her heels, expression neutral. "So the mighty Q'Mhel has fallen to the dubious charms of a puny civvie."

He lifted his hand to run it through his hair, and winced. His chest muscles felt like he'd been gored by a particularly nasty horned beast. He glanced down. Two short, metal rods protruded from his pectorals through his torn shirt, attached to wires leading to the weapon Marty had used on him. "Fryw's teat."

"An electroshock weapon, from what I can tell. The AI ran a scan on you and pinged me, since your internals were down. Those things are barbed, so it's gonna sting to dig them out."

Benar cursed under his breath. It was bad enough that his one internal, non-electric connection to his ship had triggered an automatic jump when his other systems had been overloaded. Having to take time to remove the kraden probes from his chest added insult to injury. Yasmin was in danger. He needed to move now.

With the thought of what Benfield was doing to Yasmin at that very moment pressing against his mind, Benar grabbed one of the probes and yanked it out of his chest.

Jira coughed into a fist, completely failing to hide the sardonic smile twisting her thin lips. "Might want to unplug the cartridge from the weapon first, Q'Mhel. Hate to see you get a second shock."

"Wouldn't have gotten the first if I'd been armored." He yanked the second probe out without a second thought for the pain of skin ripping. "I need to get back down there."

"You always say that."

"My woman's in danger."

Jira stood, tattooed eyebrows arched. "Gotta admit. Never heard you say that. You're serious about the civvie?"

"She's coming home with me."

"She know that?"

74

"Not yet," he admitted. She might not like it, either, but they could hash that out after he'd figured out how to save her from the winyu's ass. "AI, is Yasmin Olvera still inside her home?"

"Negative, Q'Mhel."

"AI, locate the residence of Marty Benfield. His primary home should be within a twenty-hrik radius of Yasmin's property."

Jira flipped a thumb at him. "Use antiseptic and bandages on those. I'm not treating an infection once you get back to Q space."

"Later." When Yasmin was safe.

"Do you need backup?"

"Negative. I'll relay a schedule for my return within three days, local. Start fielding jobs starting after that plus travel time. And tell the dal their vacation is over."

"And here I was looking forward to some extended leave while you play soldier boy with your little civvie." Jira returned his earlier gesture, adding a snarky grin to the insult. "Keep your net open and your boots on the ground, Q'Mhel."

"Only if I have to."

She flashed out of sight as Benar yanked his ruined shirt over his head and walked stiffly out of the room. Kraden hip replacement needed biofeedback from his neural net to function properly. There was no time to reboot it now, even if he'd had the patience for it. Armor first, then light weapons. Benfield was probably working alone, but it never hurt to be cautious. And arming quickly saved time. The AI would have the ass' residence pinpointed and jump coordinates laid in by the time Benar was ready, and as soon as he was, he'd have boots on the ground.

A neutral tone dinged and the AI said, "No residences or property registered under the name Marty Benfield have been located within the desired perimeter. Expand search criteria?"

Benar cursed under his breath. It could never be simple, could it? "AI, locate probable relatives and cross-reference their property against Benfield's likely travel routes. Expand perimeter for residence to thirty hrik. Search public databases for an address."

He ducked into his quarters and dropped his shirt onto the floor, his unaided mind formulating scenarios for Yasmin's rescue.

YASMIN THREW her entire body and all of her strength into fighting Marty. He wasn't much taller than her, but he was strong and single-minded. His grip on her arm was brutally harsh, bruising her skin. No matter how many times she yanked, he wouldn't let go. He simply dragged her off the porch and through her still-sodden yard, ignoring her efforts to resist.

As soon as they reached his car, she dropped all her weight onto the wet ground, a last ditch effort to break free. Frost-cold water seeped through her jeans, but she just didn't care. If she got into that car, there was no telling what he would do to her. "Let me go, Marty. Just let me go take care of Benar. I'll call your mother so she can come get you. We'll straighten everything out and—"

Marty twisted around and casually backhanded her across the face, never once losing his smile. "I'll forgive you for whoring around with that man, but don't say his name again."

Yasmin cupped a trembling hand to her stinging cheek and bit her lip, hard. She would not cry, no matter what he did to her. She would not cry and she would not give in.

"I'm not going with you," she said quietly. "Let go of me, Marty, and go home."

"Get in the car, Yassy. I have a great evening planned. Let's not spoil it by fighting."

She shook her head slowly. "You never were able to take no for an answer."

"You can't say no to me. You never could." He opened the back door of his sedan, yanked her off the ground, and shoved her into the backseat. "Buckle up, sweetheart. The roads are icy."

"As soon as you shut that door, I'm opening it again."

"No, you won't."

He reared back a fist and popped her hard in the jaw. Pain exploded inside her skull, and down she went, falling limply onto the plush leather upholstery, unconscious.

A soft tapping noise roused her. She shook her head, winced at the soreness radiating through her jaw, and buried her face in the soft pillow underneath her head. That oaf had really hit her. Of all the things he could've done, that one shocked her the most. Marty had never been violent with her, never even hinted at it.

Footsteps padded across a carpeted floor and a gentle hand stroked her hair. "Supper's almost ready, Yassy," Marty said. "I brought you an ice pack. I'll untie your hands if you'll be a good girl and quit trying to leave me."

Her eyes flew open and she examined her surroundings in frantic bursts. She was lying on her side on Marty's sofa in his living room. A fire burned brightly in his fireplace, adding to the soft glow of multi-colored lights strung around his Christmas tree. The nativity set she'd given him the first Christmas after they started dating was arranged just so on top of a dust-free coffee table.

Her hands and feet were tied together and her shoes were gone.

Her breath stuttered and failed, and she squeezed her eyes shut, blocking out the ever-present smile pasted on her ex-fiancé's visage. He'd hit her, kidnapped her, and trussed her like a pig ready for roasting. Worse, he'd Tased Benar and left him alone in her cabin with the door wide open.

If she'd taken Mrs. Scruggs' advice and not gone on that first lunch date, none of this would've happened.

How she could get herself out of this mess was beyond her, though. Maybe if she cooperated, Marty would eventually let down his guard and she could figure out how to escape or get to a phone and call the police. Whether they'd believe an upstanding member of the community was holding her hostage was another matter, and one she'd deal with when the time came. Hopefully, they'd at least send an ambulance out to check on Benar. That was what she had to concentrate on now, finding a way to escape so she could get help to him.

She took a deep breath, pushed it out of her lungs, and, resolved, opened her eyes and met Marty's gaze evenly. "I'll be good."

For a while, anyway.

Marty beamed at her and smacked a kiss to her forehead. "I knew you'd come around, Yassy."

True to his word, he untied her hands and feet, helped her sit upright, and pressed a cold ice pack into her hands. And because she was playing nice and needed to get to a phone, she forced a polite thank you out of her throat as she touched the ice pack to her aching jaw.

Fifteen minutes later, he led her solicitously into his immaculate formal dining room. The gleaming mahogany table was an antique, passed down through Marty's family on his mother's side. It normally seated eight. Tonight, two places were set at one end of the table. A silver candelabra held three lit taper candles, their deep red shade a perfect match to the linen placemats. Platters and tureens were carefully arranged across the rest of the table, holding enough food for a small army of guests.

Marty held her chair out for her, assisted her into it, then seated himself. "I made all your favorites."

She peered at the many dishes and chose the most polite response she could manage. "Thank you."

"It's a special time, after all. Our last Christmas Eve as an engaged couple." His hearty chuckle echoed eerily around the freshly painted room, and he winked, as if sharing a private joke. "We'll be married next year. No more abstinence. Mama is looking forward to her first grandchild, and she's not getting any younger."

Yasmin managed to choke out a hoarse, "Of course," but only just. After all these months, he still refused to believe she'd broken their engagement, was even now planning for a family. She shuddered and dropped her gaze to the antique Wedgwood chinaware. Tea roses flowed across the fine bone china, intermingled with delicately painted leaves and insects. She'd always hated these plates. They were too busy, too *rich* for her tastes.

Just like everything around her.

She glanced at Marty, happily bustling around the table dishing out food for himself. Money wasn't the problem here. She had no quarrel with folks who'd done well for themselves or even with those who'd inherited the bulk of their assets, as he had. No, the problem here was Marty. She'd never liked his house, never liked the heirlooms he surrounded himself with, never liked the pretentiousness of it all. Why had she never realized that? Why had she allowed herself to become engaged to a man so completely unsuited for her, and she for him? How could she ever have thought herself in love with him?

Benar's twitching body popped into her mind. He'd been so helpless, so pale, so unlike the strong, proud warrior she'd come to know. Queasiness roiled through her stomach, pressing upward into her chest, and a fierce pang tweaked her heart. He'd been protecting her during the past week and a half, protecting her, making love to her, sharing a sardonic humor that surprised her every single time he smiled. And he may have given her a child.

Marty set his plate down in front of his chair. "Help yourself, Yassy. I'll be back in just a minute."

He bounced out of the room into the hallway, humming "O Tennenbaum" under his breath.

She stood and locked her knees in place, stilling the trembling in her legs. Did she have time to make it to the front door? Without shoes and a jacket, would she survive outside long enough to reach the nearest neighbor?

He was back before she could make a decision, carrying his grandfather's Colt pistol. He set it on the table well out of her reach and picked up her plate. "Sorry about that. Almost forgot to get this out, in case trouble interrupts us."

It took her less than two seconds to get that by *trouble*, he really meant *Benar*. Cold horror swept through her. The Taser had been bad enough. A gun could do real, permanent damage. At the worst, it could kill, and at the very least, it could leave a scar. Her eyelids slid shut and she dropped into her chair, her imagination caught on the many scars etched into Benar's skin. Scars he'd earned in battle and training, from defending those who couldn't defend themselves or those who could afford the ridiculous prices Q set for hiring out its elite soldiers. Even the latter seemed like a more worthy cause than being shot because an ex-fiancé couldn't let go of the past.

"He's going to kill you," she blurted out, and cringed. Why had she said that? She was supposed to be playing nice, not antagonizing Marty.

He grunted and skirted around the table, spooning precise portions of steaming food onto her plate. "Has to get past the traps first. He really annoys me, you know. I left you present after present trying to show you how much I loved you, and he stole them away."

"You...what?"

"Presents, on your front porch, right where you'd find them every morning."

She stared at him open-mouthed, so shocked she couldn't speak. Marty was the one harassing her with dead animals? Harmless, never hurt a fly Marty, whose biggest sin outside of being a pretentious snob was turning down loan applications?

"Nasty man there, Yassy. That's why I had to come get you. You'd never be happy with a muscle-bound barbarian like him." He set her full plate in front of her and bussed the top of her head. "So I set a few traps. Now, eat up, sweetheart. Mama wants us to stop by after supper and open a gift."

He rambled on about all the things they were going to do together, and Yasmin let him talk, her horrified mind too numb to process his words.

CHAPTER TEN

BENAR CROUCHED outside the two-story farmhouse, studying the patterns of light glowing through the uncovered windows onto the ice-covered ground outside. It had taken far too long for the AI to track Benfield's residence, even longer for Benar to disable the traps the winyu's ass had set up around the property. Tripwires, spiked swings, even a rudimentary landmine buried off-center at the base of the steps. Child's play to dismantle or avoid, unless an untrained civilian was along for the ride.

He fully intended to leave this place with a particular untrained civvie at his side.

A shadow crossed in front of the window, too broad to be Yasmin. She was in there, though. His ship's scanners had confirmed it, though he was blind to the interior's layout without his neural net. The armor had similar sensors. They worked better interfaced with his mind, but they'd do in a pinch without the connection. Reluctantly, he activated them. Any advantage should be leveraged, regardless of how awkward it was to use.

And he'd trained for it, as every Q-hardened trainee did. With armor, without, neural net active and deactivated, and every other combination centuries of refinement could produce.

So why was his heart pounding and his breath quickened, like that of a child facing his first yinga cub?

He blinked sweat out of his eyes, cursed its presence. Yasmin. She had to be the reason behind his lack of control, her and her sweet-tart personality, her laughter and kind heart.

Her kiss.

Emotion rose swiftly, engulfing him in a tight ache centered in his chest. He loved her.

No, couldn't be. She was his lover, yes, but she was just a woman, and he...

He closed his eyes and banged a closed fist against his forehead. Jira was right. He'd fallen for Yasmin as surely as a meteor plummets toward the earth, and with the same dazzling shower of heat and light. Somehow, she'd worked her way under his skin and into his heart, a place no woman had ever held. He was hers, his heart, his life, his very blood, and she was his, whether she knew it or not.

He stood slowly in deference to his hip and aimed his handheld blaster at the landmine buried haphazardly near the steps. His finger squeezed the trigger, controlled energy burst out of the tip, travelling the short distance between him and the trap, and hit it dead on. The landmine exploded, taking part of the front steps with it, and a woman shrieked, short and piercing.

Yasmin.

His heart thumped once and turned over, then settled into the slow, steady beat he was accustomed to. His breathing leveled out and his nerves calmed, and he was once again the cold warrior his mother had bred, ruthless in his desire to save his woman.

YASMIN PUSHED her fork through the food Marty had plated for her, pretending to eat. It was beautifully prepared and probably delicious. Marty had always been a good cook, but right now, the thought of eating turned her stomach. She nodded at something he said, some half germane childhood Christmas story most likely, and pushed a forkful of plump, green peas into her sweet potato soufflé.

Had Benar woken yet? Was he even now on his way to find her or was he still lying on her living room floor, unconscious as cold air blew through the open front door into her home?

Something exploded outside, shaking the house. Yasmin shrieked and dropped her fork, and clapped her hands over her ears as she ducked in her chair. Madre de Dios, what was that?

Marty patted his mouth with his napkin, laid it carefully on the table beside his plate, and picked up the Colt. "I was afraid of this. Don't worry, sweetheart. I'll be back in just a minute and we can finish our meal in peace."

His calmness proved to be the straw that broke the camel's back. If that was Benar, as Marty seemed to believe it was, she couldn't allow that gun outside this room. Without thinking, she shoved her chair back and lunged, tackling Marty into the sturdy mahogany chair at the head of the table. He yelped and dropped the gun, and over the chair went under the force of her blow, toppling onto its side on the floor.

She let go of him instinctively, just before her arm was pinned under him and the chair. The chair's arm drove into her stomach, punching the breath out of her. She wheezed and scrambled off of Marty and under the table, well out of reach of his flailing limbs.

"What in God's name are you doing, Yassy?" he roared.

She sucked in a short breath and spat it out again. "Protecting my lover."

Marty rolled out of the chair and crawled toward the gun, laying butt end out against the glossy white floorboard. Yasmin clambered out of the table's shelter after him and grabbed his pants leg. He couldn't get that gun. That's all there was to it. It didn't matter if Benar was the one responsible for the explosion or not. Marty seemed hell bent on shooting someone, and she couldn't live with that, not when she had an opportunity to stop him.

He peered around at her over his shoulder. "Let go, Yassy. I'm warning you."

"Get away from the gun and I'll let you go."

He reared up on his knees, twisting toward her, and backhanded her, knocking her to the ground. "This is for your own good, sweetheart. You'll see."

He shook her hand off his leg and grabbed the gun, completely oblivious to the glare Yasmin aimed his way. She brushed her fingertips along her cheek and drew back blood, and her patience snapped, broken by the anger surging through her. That little verga.

He'd hit her three times in one day. Did he really think she'd let him get away with that?

He pushed himself to his feet, gun in hand, and strode past her toward the front entrance. Yasmin pulled herself upright. No, she wasn't letting him get away with it, not in any way, shape, or form. Screw compliance while waiting for a rescue party. She could save herself.

She picked up the nearest object her hand landed on and threw it at Marty's retreating back. Food sailed through the air, trailing after the plate arcing toward him. It hit him squarely along his spine, bounced off, and dropped to the floor, unbroken. Yasmin stared at it, dismayed. The least that ugly plate could've done was broken on landing.

Marty whirled around, gaping at her. "You threw my grandmother's china. That's an antique, Yassy. What were you thinking?"

"I was thinking that I always hated that china," she said flatly, and picked up his bread plate and lobbed it at his head. It sailed past him and crashed into the doorframe, shattering into dozens of pieces. "In fact, I hope to God I never see this stupid chinaware again."

"Now, Yassy."

She lobbed object after object at him as she spoke, uncaring of what she picked up, silverware, china, the placemat. "That. Is. Not. My. Name."

He cursed under his breath as he ducked and wove around her poorly aimed pitches. Food splattered everywhere, on his forest green cashmere sweater, on the Oriental rug under the table, on the walls, and Yasmin didn't care. She was sick to death of Marty Benfield and all his nonsense, just sick of it. For years, she'd kowtowed and simpered. She'd bit her tongue and endured endless conversations with his snotty relatives, his sweet mother excluded, bless her, and she'd just had it. No more! Not one drop more would Yasmin take.

Thank goodness Benar wasn't like that.

As if her thoughts had conjured him, he stepped into the hallway behind Marty, wearing dull gray armor covering him from his neck to the tips of his toes and fingers. He arched a black eyebrow at her.

"Need help?"

Marty whipped around, raising the gun, and Yasmin's heart froze. No, not Benar. Not him. At that close of a range, a bullet would surely pierce his armor no matter what it was made of. It would kill him, just when they'd found each other. Against all odds, in a universe so vast they should never have met, they'd found love.

And that was something worth fighting for.

She picked up the nearest object and leapt toward Marty. Warm liquid dribbled down her arm as she raised the antique Wedgwood gravy bowl and smashed it into the back of his head. He crumpled to the ground, out cold, and she staggered back, half appalled at the violence of her own actions.

Benar grunted. "Put on my armor for nothing, looks like."

A laugh burst out of her, borderline hysterical. She stumbled into his outstretched arms, blinking back tears, and cuddled against the smooth armor protecting him from everything but her heart. "I was so scared, Benar. I thought you were really hurt."

"Just for a while, beauty," he said gently. "Ready to go home?"

"You have no idea," she said, and lifted on her tiptoes and kissed him soundly, the hero who'd charged to her rescue, even if in the end she hadn't needed him to. She dropped back onto her feet and smoothed her hands over his face. "What do we do with this bozo?"

"I'll take care of it," he said in that gruff, guttural voice of his, and she kissed him again, just because she could.

CHAPTER ELEVEN

BENAR JUMPED HIMSELF, Yasmin, and a trussed up Benfield into her yard, out of view of the cabin's windows. While he'd been tying up a groggy winyu's ass and Yasmin had cleaned broken dishes and food off the floor, the sensors he'd installed around her home had gone off.

Someone was in her house, five someones, by the AI's count.

He dropped Benfield face first into the frosty yard, then tugged a borrowed jacket more closely around Yasmin's shoulders. "Stay here. No arguments."

She nodded, oddly demure, and accepted the kiss he pressed to the tip of her brave nose without comment.

His woman was a warrior, not the helpless child he'd thought her when they'd first met. She hadn't needed his help subduing her captor, proof that she'd do well at the Choosing, once he'd refined her aim a bit.

He allowed a small smile to curve his mouth into humor as he engaged his face shield on transparent and approached the cabin. Five humans were inside, three near the fire, two in the kitchen area. At least they'd shut the door when they'd entered.

He yanked out a second weapon, aimed both away from his body, and triggered a jump into the verge of the hallway, facing the front entrance, between the two groups of humans. Five surprised Earthlings whirled toward him, hands reaching for weapons. He aimed his own at them and said, "Stop."

Immediately, all five did, raising their hands in the air, palms out. A man on his left stepped into view, and Benar recognized Valentin, wearing Yasmin's apron over immaculately maintained dress clothes. Ritual tattoos peeked from behind an open collar and sleeves rolled to mid-arm, black splotches of ink on dusky skin.

"We came to pay our holiday respects to our brother's sister," Valentin said. "I was alarmed to find her door open and her home empty."

Benar grunted. "She was kidnapped."

Valentin nodded. "My men are out searching for her."

"Call them off."

"You found her?"

Benar shook his head slowly, unable to contain his grin. "I found her, but she'd already saved herself."

"And the one who took her?"

"Rendered harmless."

Valentin twitched a hand toward his pants pocket. "My men?"

Benar lowered his guns. These men were dangerous, yes, but not to Yasmin, not at the moment. Meanwhile, she was standing outside in the freezing cold waiting for him to clear the house. "Why are you really here?"

Valentin retrieved his phone and passed it to the man on his right, who dialed a number and turned his back on them. "Angelina said Yasmin was being harassed."

Benar bit back a curse. That little yinga *had* been spying on Yasmin. It would break her heart to learn it. She'd grown fond of the spitfire child and given her a place at the shop, sweeping floors and running errands. "Yasmin's former fiancé believed he could have her still."

"Not very bright," Valentin said, his accented voice mild. "You set him straight."

"She did."

"Good. She's safe?"

"She is."

"Then our work here is done." Valentin untied the apron and slid it over his head, folded it and placed it neatly on the counter next to the celery Yasmin had been chopping. "Should you need my aid—"

"We won't," Benar said flatly.

Valentin nodded and rolled his shirtsleeves down, buttoned them tightly against his wrists. "Feliz Navidad."

The men murmured polite goodbyes as they left, bowing their heads respectfully toward Benar. Valentin shrugged on his coat and said, his expression neutral, "You're not from here."

It wasn't a question, and so Benar let it stand. Better for this man, who already held enough power over Yasmin and her family, to never know the truth of Benar's origins.

Valentin nodded once and exited. Benar followed him out, watching patiently as the five men entered the two vehicles parked at the end of Yasmin's driveway and left. As soon as they were out of sight, he strode through the night-swept yard toward Yasmin, allowing the thin moonlight to guide his steps.

She was standing over Benfield, watching him dispassionately, bouncing slightly as she huddled in her jacket. "All clear?"

"Valentin and his men. They're gone now."

"Can we go inside?"

"Go on. I'll be back in a moment."

She jerked her stubborn chin at Benfield. "What are you going to do with him?"

"Put him in the brig for the night."

"Shouldn't we call the police?"

"Will they punish him?"

She shook her head wearily and her eyes dropped to her toes. "I don't think anything will happen to him. Maybe if we'd called them while we were still at his house."

Inherited property, still held in his family's name, the reason it had taken so long for Benar to track the ass down. "Justice would be swift and merciless on Q."

"You can't take him there. People will notice him missing. I'll be the first person they point their fingers at."

Not if she wasn't on Earth, but it was a salient point. "What do you suggest?"

She shrugged and rubbed the tip of her cold-reddened nose. "I don't know. Maybe we should've given him to Valentin."

Benar grinned and chucked her chin. "That can be arranged."

She laughed as he'd intended her to and trudged through slush into her home. Benar grabbed a shivering Benfield by the back of his sweater and dragged him onto the front porch. He retrieved a jump chip from a crevice in his armor and affixed it to the man, waited while the AI calculated a moving jump from there into Valentin's vehicle, then triggered it. Those moving jumps didn't always work out exactly correctly. Sometimes, the anticipated landing coordinates were off just a shade, enough to, say, place the jumper under the targeted landing site instead of inside it.

Too bad for Benfield. Either way, they were rid of him and could enjoy their last night on Earth in peace.

CHRISTMAS MORNING dawned bright and early. Yasmin yawned and stretched, sliding one bare foot down Benar's muscled leg. She had a full day planned. Gifts to open, Christmas mass, visits with friends and family in the afternoon, and at the end of the day, cuddling up next to Benar.

He was bound to leave any day now. There was nothing keeping him here, now that Marty was safely away from her. A sharp pang stole her breath and she turned her face into Benar's chest, nuzzling the soft mat of hair covering his firm pectorals. He was leaving her. Nothing she could do about it, but she could enjoy the time they had left without regrets for what might've been.

He stirred beneath her cheek and murmured, "Myengen dun arig."

"Merry Christmas, Benar."

He snorted softly. "You must learn Pruxnæ, beauty."

She laughed and kissed his chest, teasing him. He rolled her onto her back and slid into her, and her laughter turned to encouraging sighs and moans and muted laughter as they made slow, sweet love.

The day continued exactly as she'd planned. They showered

together in her tiny bathroom, then she led Benar to the Christmas tree and gave him her gift.

He held the brightly wrapped package in his strong, capable hands for long moments, staring down at it with a blank expression. "You have given me so much, beauty. Another gift was not necessary."

"It's part of our tradition," she said simply. "A token of my affection for you, and my appreciation. I don't know what I would've done about Marty if you hadn't been here."

"That I did for my brother." He turned the small package over, examining it from every angle. "You truly feel affection for me?"

So much, he'd never know. More than she could possibly share, given the short time they'd known each other. "Yes."

He raised his dark gaze slowly to hers. "I have no gift for you save what I hold in my heart."

"Oh, Benar." She cupped his smooth jaws in her hands, gently tracing her thumbs along his high cheekbones. "It's ok, really. I know you have to leave. You don't have to say anything to make me feel better about it."

"I am leaving, yes." He set her gift aside and gathered her close, holding her tightly against his broad chest. "But I'm not going alone."

Before she could process his words, the world turned in a quick circle of distorted light and winked out, and she fell into darkness, safe in his arms.

She woke alone, chained to a bed in a Spartan room she recognized immediately. Benar's bedroom on his ship. He'd kidnapped her, the second man to do so in two days. The notion tickled her to the core and laughter bubbled up and over, spilling into the stark room, bouncing against its gray walls. What a prize she must be, then. Rachel would get a hoot out of it, if no one else did, and surely, she was the only person from Earth who'd believe Yasmin's story.

Benar ducked into the room and halted just across the threshold. "I've never heard tale of a woman laughing when a Pruxnæ male has kidnapped her for his bride."

"Well, there's a first time for everything." She jiggled her hands, rattling chains. "What am I doing chained to your bed? You could've asked me to sleep with you here."

"You're not there to sleep, woman. You're there to please your future mate."

"My mate," she repeated slowly, and hope rose so swiftly, it choked her breath. "You want me to be your wife?"

His expression softened and he was no longer the proud warrior, a Q'Mhel among his people. He was the man she'd fallen in love with, the man whose child she might carry, and the man whose heart she hoped she held.

He crossed the room and sat down beside her, one hand resting on her stomach, warming her through the blanket he'd draped over her. "I love you, beauty. I know you care for me. In time, you will come to love me as a wife should, but first, you will fight for me in the Choosing and earn your place at my side."

"Haven't I already?" she murmured. "Isn't loving you enough?"

"Love." His hand splayed against her stomach and he glanced away. "You love me truly?"

"Yes, Benar. I do. And I want to be your wife, but I can't just abandon my home and my shop."

"I called Esme," he admitted gruffly. "While you were recovering from the sedative I gave you before we jumped."

"You drugged me?"

"Only to ease your transition to life shipboard. You will forgive me."

It wasn't a plea, and for some reason, it tickled her something fierce. She managed to keep a straight face around her laughter. "I will, as soon as you unchain me."

A wicked smile flashed across his handsome face. "I have plans, beauty. Indulge me, just this once."

"I really need to check on my shop."

He stretched out beside her, tracing the line of her hip with his fingers through the blanket. "Esme is handling it. Ernest has promised to watch over your home. Your family will be contacted and I gathered enough clothing to last for the duration of our trip."

It seemed he'd thought of everything, then, including knowing exactly what she needed in order to feel comfortable being with him. "What if I wasn't ready to leave?"

"We will return. Later." He turned her face toward his and kissed her gently, silencing her protests. "Trust me, beauty. Everything will work out as it should. I love you."

His quietly spoken words filled her, joining the love she held for him blooming inside her heart. They were just starting their journey together, here on his ship, and she hoped it would be a long one, full of laughter and light, and love shared in the touch of a warrior who had saved her in more ways than she could count.

GLOSSARY

Ceg. A unit of measure used by the Pruxnæ, roughly eighteen Terran inches.

Tick. One second or a moment.

Umlek. An inexact measurement. Approximately twelve.

Vud. An Abywian monetary unit. At current exchange rates, one vud is equivalent to 1.245 Galactic credits.

THE PRUXNÆ SERIES

Thief of Hearts

Queen's Guard Alna Lomig is on the verge of fulfilling her destiny, until she's kidnapped by handsome Pruxnæ Gared ab Einif, who has other plans for his Lady Warrior.

The Choosing

Ziri Mokuru was looking for her place in the wide, wide universe. Ryn abid Alna knew exactly where she belonged: In his heart.

Alien Mine

Dyuvad ab Mhij journeys into Origin Space to the home of Rachel Hunter, the mother of a young girl Dyuvad must protect at the behest of a mysterious Net telepath.

Sweet Surrender

Tyelu af Alna meets her match in mercenary-soldier Jos Q'Mhel.

About the Author

Lucy Varna lives in the Blue Ridge Mountains of northeast Georgia, surrounded by her large, extended family.

Visit her online at:
www.lucyvarna.com

Learn more about the Pruxnæ:
www.lucyvarna.com/netverse.html

Also available from Lucy Varna

THE DAUGHTERS OF THE PEOPLE SERIES
The Prophecy
Light's Bane
The Enemy Within
Tempered
In All Things, Balance
Sanctuary

THE SONS OF THE PEOPLE SERIES
Say Yes

THE CULLOWHEE HERITAGE SERIES
A Higher Purpose
A Wicked Love